THE CASE OF THE SMUGGLER'S CURSE

THE FIRST AFTER SCHOOL DETECTIVE CLUB
MYSTERY

F.S. DAWSON

Illustrated by
STUART BACHE

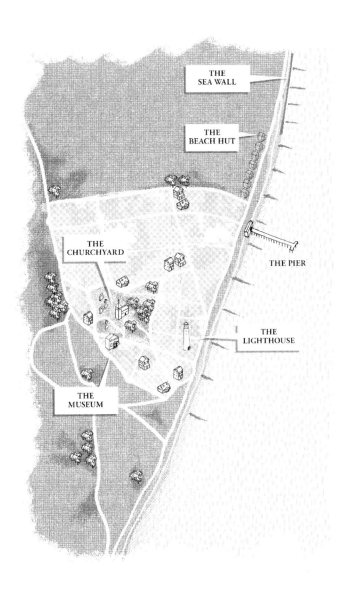

THE
SEA WALL

THE
BEACH HUT

THE PIER

THE
CHURCHYARD

THE
LIGHTHOUSE

THE
MUSEUM

1

STRANGERS

Lucy Yeung pounded her way up the hill, gritting her teeth as she forced her tired legs to their limit. She sucked down cold gasps of winter air that burned her lungs, and she lengthened her stride to take in the slope without losing pace.

At the top of the hill she could see her goal, a neat terraced house with bright blue paint and a pretty garden that was her mother's pride and joy. Only a few more yards now, she told herself. She fixed her eyes on the warm yellow light spilling from the windows and put on an extra burst of speed, thinking of hot soup and warm showers.

Standing at the garden gate was a tall man, lean and fit, frowning at something he held in his hand. Lucy's father was always there with the stopwatch when she finished a training run. And he was usually unhappy with what it told him.

She sprinted the last few yards and slapped her hand down on the gatepost as her father clicked off the watch.

"How was that?" she said triumphantly.

Her father frowned at the numbers on the dial like he

did when he was displeased. "Not good, Lucy," he said. "What is this? You're nearly a whole three seconds slower than yesterday. Are you getting lazy on me?"

"I'm not lazy," said Lucy with a frown. "It's just that I've been working hard at school all week. And you made me go for a run this morning. *And* I still have homework to do. And on top of all that, you still want me to run faster than I did yesterday."

Her father's face darkened, and he raised a stern eyebrow in that way of his that always made her feel guilty. She began to regret her outburst.

"You only get one chance in life, Lucy," he said sternly. "I had a chance to run for my country when I was thirteen, just like you. I was good. I could have made it all the way to the Olympics."

Lucy sighed and kicked the toe of her trainers against the garden wall. She had heard this story a lot of times. "I'm sorry, Dad," she said. "I'll try to do better next time." She flicked a strand of long dark hair out of her eyes and shivered. Now that she had stopped running, she was feeling the cold.

"Trying isn't good enough, Lucy," snapped her father. "If you want to be an Olympian, then you have to make up your mind that you're going to do it, whatever it takes. I wasted my opportunity because I didn't have anyone to show me how to use my talents. I don't want you to make the same mistake."

Lucy nodded. "I'll do it better tomorrow, Dad," she said. "I promise."

His father shook his head. "Not tomorrow, Lucy," he said. "*Tonight.* Do the circuit again."

Lucy groaned. "Oh, come on, Dad! It's cold and I'm tired. My times will be all over the place."

His father held up a warning finger that meant no further arguments would be heard on the subject. "Tired doesn't cut it," he said. "That's just an excuse. And while you're running, you can think about what it means to be truly dedicated." He handed her the stopwatch. "You can time yourself on this circuit. I have other things I need to do. Now – off you go." He turned back to the house.

Lucy knew it was useless to argue. For a moment, she thought about going inside to appeal to her mother, who always took a more lenient view of her daughter's training than her husband. But, in the end, she decided it would only cause an argument, and it would just be easier to complete the extra circuit.

With a last, longing look at the welcoming light from the hallway, she began to run again, trying to force some warmth back into her muscles. Sometimes her dad could be a real pain.

Joe found his mother in her usual place, sitting at her dressing table and looking into the mirror. Penelope Carter continued applying her eye make-up with expert attention to detail, unaware she was being watched. When she caught sight of Joe hovering in the doorway, she flinched in surprise, smudging her mascara. Then she frowned with annoyance.

"Did you want something, Joe?" she asked, deftly removing the smudge with a cotton bud.

"I was just wondering – have you heard from Dad yet?"

His mother sighed impatiently. Joe did not know if she was annoyed by the smudge or by his question, but she was *definitely* annoyed. "He's not coming home," she said, starting to apply her make-up again. "Not for a couple of weeks, anyway. This business trip is very important to him, and he still has a lot to do."

"A couple of weeks?" Joe could not keep the disappointment from his voice. "But that means he won't be home for Christmas!"

Penelope Carter sighed again and put down her make-up brush. She turned to look at him with an expression that meant he was about to get a lecture. "Your father is an important man," she said. "He works very hard and makes a lot of sacrifices so we can live in this lovely big house and you can have all those nice things in your bedroom. Would you rather not have those things, Joe? Would you?"

Joe pushed his shoulder-length blond hair back off his face and shrugged. "Well...I suppose not..."

"There you are, then. You're eleven now, Joe. You should be able to deal with life's little disappointments." She turned back to the mirror and began primping her hair.

Joe hesitated. "So, if Dad's not coming home, perhaps you and I could do something together at the weekend?"

"Do something?" His mother frowned. "Like what?"

"I don't know. Watch a movie or something?" He brightened. "Or perhaps we could take out the motorboat?"

His mother laughed lightly, and he thought how pretty her laugh sounded. "I don't have time for movies," she said. "And as for that wretched boat, are you serious? In this weather? You know how seasick I get. I'm sorry, Joe, but I just don't have the time right now. Your father will be home in two weeks, and we'll celebrate Christmas together then. Now run along, there's a darling. I have cocktails at the Benfleets' in half an hour, and I'm going to be late."

Joe sighed and trudged wearily back to his room. He knew he shouldn't have got his hopes up. His father's job meant they were seldom together at Christmas, but it would have been nice, just for once.

He sat on his bed and looked around his room, at the model planes hanging from the ceiling, the remote-controlled drone his father had sent him for his birthday, and at the expensive computer sitting on his desk. It was true, he did have nice things, but he would happily have given them all up if it meant they could be together.

There was a knock at the door, and his mother swished in, wearing her best winter coat. "I've left you something in the microwave, and there's some of those sausage rolls you like in the fridge. Do your homework, and don't go to bed late. I should be home by midnight. Bye."

She bent down to air-kiss him so that she didn't smudge her make-up. Then she swished out again, leaving only a cloud of expensive fragrance behind her.

Joe lay back and thought about eating another microwave dinner on his own. If only there was someone he could spend the evening with. But he had no brothers or sisters, and he didn't have many friends, either.

It had been nearly six months since they had moved to this house. It had been his father's idea to live by the seaside, even though he was hardly ever at home and his mother seemed to hate everything to do with the sea.

Joe had discovered quite quickly that most of the kids in his new school already knew each other very well, and they spent a lot of free time going to each other's houses. But his mother had never been very keen on him bringing his friends back to their house, so he seemed destined to spend his evenings alone.

He sat up and stroked his chin, the way that people did in books when they were having an idea. It was all very well having nice things, he thought, but it didn't mean much if you had no friends to share them with, did it? And he was hardly going to make friends sitting here by himself, was he?

Joe began to pace up and down the room. There was no point in trying to make friends here in Southwold. He'd been trying to do that ever since they had moved here, with no luck. No, if he was going to make friends, he was going to have to go further afield. And that meant he was going to have to pack a bag.

Moving quickly, he reached under the bed for his rucksack, then started to rummage in the wardrobe for the clothes he would need.

Joe was going on a journey!

2

ON THE BEACH

Max Green stepped out onto the cold pavement and shivered in the icy night air. He waved goodnight to his after-school tutor, then pulled up his hood and slung his rucksack across his shoulders. A frown creased the brown skin of his forehead as he felt the first spatters of rain. He enjoyed having extra lessons with his tutor, but he hated coming home in the dark, especially in winter.

Max liked living by the sea in summer, when the days were endless and there was nothing to do except to swim and lie on the beach. But winter by the sea was a whole different ball game. The sea wind got right inside your duffel coat, the rain fogged your glasses, and there was nothing to do but to wait for the warm weather. Southwold in winter was like the evil twin of Southwold in summer.

As he walked up North Parade, a noise up ahead made him stop, peering into the darkness through his rain-spattered glasses. A group of older boys were hanging about on the street corner, laughing and pushing each other around playfully. Max recognised them immediately. Toby Watts and his mates. Max bit his lip. If he carried on, he would have to walk right past them.

It'll be fine, he told himself. *Just look straight ahead and keep going, they probably won't even notice you.* Except it never really worked out that way, did it? He knew from bitter experience that Toby Watts and his gorillas *always* noticed him. There was something about Max that attracted their attention the way that blood in the water attracted sharks.

And after they'd noticed him, well...then anything might happen. If he was lucky, it might just be a bit of name-calling. 'Micro-nerd' seemed to be their favourite term of abuse at the moment. If he was less lucky, he might get pushed around or have his books dropped in a puddle or...or worse. Best not to take the chance.

He turned around and started to walk the other way. It was a long detour back to his house, but it was safer in the long run. He had not gone far when he paused for a second time. Someone else was coming towards him along the promenade from the direction of the pier: a girl, tall and dark haired with a swinging ponytail. Her long legs pounded a regular rhythm on the pavement as she ran. Max smiled when he recognised her and breathed a sigh of relief. It was only Lucy.

The girl broke into a broad grin as she approached. "Hey, Max," she called. "Aren't you done with all the studying yet?"

"I don't know, Luce," he called back. "Aren't you done with all the running yet?"

She laughed in a good-natured way; then she fell into step beside him. "And what," she said in mock horror, "is that?"

She leaned across him and hooked her finger under his tie, flipping it out of his jacket in a single movement. Max frowned and tucked his tie back in, smoothing it down carefully. His old-fashioned dress sense and his fondness for ties were a never-ending source of amusement for Lucy.

"It's important to be well turned out," he said with a sniff. "You never get a second chance to make a first impression."

"That tie looks like something my dad would wear," said Lucy. "Where on earth do you buy that stuff?"

"Nerds-R-Us," said Max, straight-faced. "It's where all the best losers go to shop."

A puzzled look crossed Lucy's face. "Aren't you going in the wrong direction? Your house is that way."

"Thought I'd take the long way home," he said breezily. "I need the exercise."

Lucy didn't say anything. She glanced back at the boys gathered on the street corner, and Max wondered if she'd guessed the truth.

He looked up at the girl. Even though they were a similar age, she was at least a head taller. "Aren't you going to mess up your running times walking with me?" he said, knowing how strict Lucy's father could be.

Lucy shrugged. "Nah, I already did my timed run tonight. The old man made me go around again for being slow."

"Why don't you just take a shortcut?" said Max. "If it were me, I'd miss out a few streets and be home in record-breaking time."

Lucy looked shocked. "Because that would be cheating. And cheats never win in the long run. Besides" – she held up a hand to show the large device strapped to her wrist – "Dad always checks my GPS when I get home."

Max snorted. "You should give me that thing. I could fix it so your dad would never know."

Lucy grinned again. "Thanks, but no. By the way, thanks for helping me with my maths homework last week. I got an A. That's the best I've done all term."

Max shrugged. "No sweat. Now if you could just do PE for me, we'd be even."

Lucy laughed. "I'm sure you'd enjoy sports a lot more if you just tried a little bit. How about a quick walk along the beach before we head home? Get some fresh air into those geeky lungs of yours."

"If you insist."

Max made a face, but secretly he was pleased to have met up with his friend. For one thing he found her easy to talk to, and he always felt relaxed in her company, not like he did with most other people. For another, having an athlete like Lucy by your side tended to make the bullies think twice.

She peered up at the sky as they walked towards the steps that led down to the beach. "Do you think it will be a white Christmas this year?"

"Don't be ridiculous." Max laughed. "They only put snow on Christmas cards to get everyone in the holiday mood. It never snows at Christmas, at least not here. It just rains."

He realised that Lucy had stopped walking and was looking at a bus stop a short way up the road. Max followed her gaze and saw a solitary figure sitting inside, a gangly boy with shoulder-length blond hair plastered down by the rain. He seemed to be crying.

"Do you think he's okay?" asked Lucy.

Max shrugged. "I think I recognise him from school. He's one of the new kids in year seven."

"Year seven?" said Lucy. "Were we really that small last year?"

"In case you hadn't noticed, some of us are still that small," said Max drily.

Lucy didn't reply. She walked over to the boy. "Are you okay?"

Joe Carter looked up in surprise at the very tall Chinese girl and the very short Black boy now standing in front of him. He had got soaked on his way to the bus stop and had then discovered that there were no more buses until morning. Realising that his plan to run away and make new friends seemed to be over before it had begun, he had sat down and begun to cry.

He jumped up quickly, rubbing his eyes. "I wasn't crying. It's just the rain, that's all."

"If you say so," said Lucy. She looked at the boy curiously. His clothes all carried expensive-looking labels, but they were completely unsuitable for the wet weather.

Max nodded at the timetable on the bus-shelter wall. "No more buses tonight."

"Oh." Joe glanced around quickly. "Yes, I know. I'm just waiting for...for some friends!" He brightened. "Yes, they'll be by any moment to pick me up, and then we're all going to a big party. I have lots of friends. I have so many friends I don't know what to do with them all." He gave an unconvincing laugh.

"We'll take your word for it," said Lucy. "Well, if you're sure you're okay, goodnight, then."

Max and Lucy turned away, but the boy started after them. "Wait!" he said quickly. "Perhaps I could come with you guys instead?"

"What about your friends?" said Max.

The boy slung the rucksack over his shoulder and fell into step behind them. "Don't worry, they won't mind. So, where are we going?"

Max and Lucy exchanged a glance. "Nowhere special," said Max. "Just the beach. It's not as exciting as going to a party."

"That's okay," said the boy. "I wasn't much in the mood for a party, anyway."

Max rolled his eyes, and Lucy shrugged, but neither of them quite had the heart to tell the boy to go away, so they just let him follow them.

They descended the steps to the empty beach, feeling their feet sink into the soft, damp sand. They turned left and passed beneath the old pier as they walked away from the town. The great iron structure was now dark for the winter and looking like the skeleton of some vast sea monster that had washed up on the shore. The rain had begun to ease a little, and Lucy took a lungful of the fresh, clean air. White-topped breakers sloshed around the iron girders of the pier and crashed onto the sand in the darkness. Coming here reminded Lucy that the peaceful little town in which she lived was still on the very edge of a wild and dangerous sea. It was the part of the beach she liked best of all.

"It's beautiful here, don't you think?" she said.

"I prefer it in the summer," said Max.

"I know you two!" said Joe, still behind them. "You're Lucy Yeung. You won the 1500 metres in the interschool tournament last month."

Lucy flashed him a quick smile.

"And you're Max Green. You're the school chess champion."

"Three years running," said Max. "What did you say your name was?"

"Joe. Joe Carter." He held out his hand.

Max looked at the hand for a moment and then gave it a quick shake. "Charmed."

They left the pier behind and walked along a row of colourful wooden beach huts, painted in brilliant shades of yellow, red and turquoise. "The rain's stopped," said Lucy. "Shall we sit down for a bit?" She was resigned to the fact that this strange boy wasn't going away any time soon and, besides, she loved sitting on the beach at night and just watching the waves.

Lucy approached one of the beach huts and brushed the sand from the wooden steps, sitting down in the shelter of the overhanging roof. Max sat beside her, and Joe sat on the other side, grinning at his two new-found friends.

"Hey," he said, rummaging in his rucksack. "Does anyone fancy a sausage roll? I brought some for the journey." He pulled a limp pastry roll from his bag and offered it to Max and Lucy. It looked battered and slightly damp, and they both shook their heads politely. Joe shrugged and took a bite, spilling pastry crumbs down the front of his shirt.

"What journey?" said Max after a while. "I thought you said you were going to a party."

For a moment Joe looked confused. "Oh, that." He laughed, spraying more crumbs. "No, that wasn't really true." He took another bite and then spoke with his mouth full. "I was running away."

"Running away?" Lucy's eyes widened. "You mean like running away from home?"

"Sure," said Joe. He crammed the last piece of sausage roll in his mouth and reached into the bag for another. "I wanted to find some new friends. But hey." He looked up and grinned. "I don't need to worry now that I've found you."

Max and Lucy stared at the boy open mouthed for a moment. Max was about to say that they weren't his friends when they were interrupted by a loud barking coming from further down the beach.

"Now what?" grumbled Max.

A small dog was running along the sand towards them, barking frantically as he came. The dog had short legs and a barrel chest. He was mostly white with brown patches on his head and floppy ears. He scampered straight past Lucy and Max and came to a stop in front of Joe, still barking madly.

"He's got a big bark for such a small dog," said Lucy.

"I think he likes me," said Joe, evidently pleased to have made another friend.

"Don't flatter yourself," said Max. "I think he just likes sausage rolls."

Joe broke off a piece of sausage and threw it to the dog, who caught it in mid-air, throwing back his head to wolf it down in a single gulp. No sooner had the dog swallowed the piece than he started barking again.

"Now you've done it," said Lucy. "You'll never get rid of him now."

This news clearly delighted Joe, who began tearing off more pieces of sausage roll and throwing them to the dog. He laughed hysterically each time the animal successfully caught a piece in his jaws. "He's so scruffy looking." Joe laughed. "I bet he doesn't have an owner. Perhaps I should take him home."

No sooner had Joe spoken than there was a yell from along the beach. "What do you idiots think you're doing?"

They turned to see a girl stalking out of the gloom towards them. She was short and very slight, with pale skin and brown hair tied in two long plaits, and a pair of battered binoculars hung around her neck.

Despite her small size, she wore an expression of complete fury. Her teeth were bared, and her eyebrows were knitted together in a furious scowl. Her fists were clenched into bloodless knots, and she was glaring directly at Joe as she stomped up the beach.

"I think you just found his owner," said Max. "And she doesn't look too pleased with you."

Joe gulped and instinctively moved to a higher step as the girl came marching towards him. "Oh no!" he gasped. "I know her. It's crazy Charlotte Wells."

3

WRECKERS

L ucy watched the advancing girl cautiously. "I've seen her around at school," she said. "She's always sitting in the playground by herself."

"That's because everyone's afraid of her," said Joe in an urgent whisper. "She's always going on about birds and wildlife and saving the planet and stuff like that, but she seems to hate people. Last month a boy in our class threw a stone at a seagull, and she got so angry that she punched him on the nose and made it bleed. She's crazy, I tell you."

"Great, that's all we need." Max sighed. "A runaway *and* a crazy person."

As the girl drew closer, she started shouting again. "What are you doing feeding my dog!" she yelled. "He's not yours. You've got no right. How dare you!"

Max blinked in surprise. He did not think he had ever seen anyone look as angry as Charlotte Wells seemed to be right now. Her face was screwed up in a furious scowl, her fists were clenched tightly, and her eyes flashed with fire. She looked like a small animal that was preparing to fight to the death.

Joe backed into the porch of the beach hut, with his hands held out in front of him defensively. "I didn't mean anything by it," he stammered. "I just gave him a bit of sausage, that's all. He liked it. It's good for him."

"Cheap and nasty sausage rolls are *not* good for him," raged the girl. "Or anyone else for that matter."

"They're not cheap," protested Joe. "My mum buys them special. They're organic. It says on the packet that–"

"I don't care what they are," yelled the girl. "*I* take care of my dog, and no one else feeds him except for me. Got that?"

Joe was nodding frantically. "S-sure," he spluttered. "Anything you say."

"I'm sure Joe didn't mean any harm," said Lucy. "He just didn't understand. Did you, Joe?"

Joe shook his head vigorously, still trying to keep as far away from Charlotte Wells as possible.

"There you are," said Lucy. "So why don't you two make up and be friends?"

"Yeah," said Max. "Joe needs friends. And you both seem to get on so well together."

Lucy shot Max a glare, and he shut up immediately.

Charlotte Wells folded her arms and clamped her mouth into a tight line. She narrowed her eyes at Lucy, and the older girl returned her gaze unflinchingly. "Alright, I'll let him off this time," she said eventually. She jabbed an accusing finger at Joe, who flinched visibly. "But *he'd* better not come near my dog again." She turned to her dog, who now seemed to be barking wildly into the darkness. "Come on, Sherlock," she said. "It's time to go."

"Your name's Charlotte, isn't it?" asked Lucy as the girl turned to go.

The girl turned back and glared at Lucy with fresh venom in her eyes. "Don't *ever* call me *Charlotte*," she said through gritted teeth. "No one calls me that. My name's Charlie. C-H-A-R-L-I-E. Got that?"

"Alright, alright," said Lucy, sounding annoyed. "I was just trying to be friendly, that's all."

"I don't need friends. Me and Sherlock do just fine together."

"Yeah, you seem well suited," said Max. "Sherlock's already off picking a fight with someone else." They all looked at the little dog, who was facing away from them and still barking angrily.

"Is he always like that?" said Lucy.

"No," said Charlie, with a puzzled frown. "I don't know what's got into him. He's usually so well behaved. Hey, Sherlock, cut it out!" She bent down and tapped him lightly on the rump, but it made no difference. The little dog kept barking as though his life depended on it.

"I think there's someone over there," said Joe, pointing. "Up on those rocks. I think that's who Sherlock's barking at."

A hundred metres up the beach from where they were sitting, the beach huts came to an end and the sea wall began. As tall as two people, the wall formed a grim concrete and stone barrier against the vicious winter storms that would otherwise have hit the town like a hammer.

Directly in front of the sea wall, hundreds of large granite blocks had been piled up in long lines extending straight out into the sea. Lucy knew from school that the granite blocks were there to reduce the force of the waves and stop them from damaging the wall. She also knew that the blocks were uneven and slippery and that it was dangerous to stand on them.

Now that their eyes had adjusted to the darkness, they could see a dark figure standing on top of one of the long lines of blocks, right near the farthest end of the sea wall.

The waves crashed furiously around him, and he was getting covered in spray, but he seemed to be taking no notice.

"What's he doing?" said Lucy. "It's really dangerous to stand up there. He could get washed away."

"Do you think he's in trouble?" asked Joe. "Maybe we should see if we can help?"

"He's holding something," said Max, "but I can't see what it is."

Charlie seemed to have forgotten her anger from a moment ago. She raised her binoculars and peered at the man. "Looks like he's holding a lamp of some sort."

As she spoke, a flame flickered, and a yellow glow bloomed in the darkness. "It *is* a lamp," said Lucy. "I think he's signalling to someone."

The figure had begun to wave his lantern back and forth so that it really did look like he was giving some kind of signal. But there didn't appear to be anyone else on the beach, apart from them, who could see it.

"Look," said Max, pointing out to sea. "There's a ship out there."

Far out in the blackness, a faint light blinked on and off several times, as though it was answering the glow from the stranger's lamp. "I know what he's doing," said Joe breathlessly. He hopped up and down on the boards excitedly. "He's a wrecker."

Lucy gave him a puzzled look. "What's a wrecker?"

"I read about them," gasped Joe. "They used to stand on the shoreline and shine lights to lure boats onto the rocks so that they'd get wrecked. Then the wreckers would steal everything they could from the boat and leave the poor crew to drown. That's what wreckers do."

"A hundred years ago, maybe," said Max. "But I never heard about there being any wreckers in modern times."

"Well, he's doing something odd," said Lucy. All the talk of wreckers had aroused her curiosity, and the man did seem to be behaving very strangely. "Perhaps we should take a closer look?"

"Sherlock!" yelled Charlie suddenly. "Sherlock, come back here!"

The little dog had been barking continuously at the stranger and had now decided that this was something he needed to investigate. Without waiting for permission from his mistress, he bolted suddenly across the sand, heading straight for the strange man on the rocks.

"Sherlock!" cried Charlie again. There was a note of fear in her voice. "Come back! You'll get hurt." She took off after Sherlock, sprinting along the sand as fast as she could run.

Lucy stood up. "Maybe we should go too," she said quickly. "They might need help."

Max was quite pleased that Charlie had gone, and he

was about to say so, but Lucy had already set off in pursuit of the girl and her little dog.

"Wait for me!" cried Joe. He skipped down the steps after Lucy and ran after her.

Max watched them go and then rolled his eyes. "That's just great," he muttered to himself. Then he clambered wearily to his feet. "Wait up, you guys," he called. "I can't run that fast." He began a slow, shuffling jog across the sand.

Lucy's long legs gave her the advantage, and she quickly caught up with Charlie. They reached the sea wall at the same time, with Joe arriving a few moments later. Charlie quickly grabbed Sherlock by the collar and held on to prevent him bolting again. By the time Max arrived, puffing and blowing, they were all standing in the shadows, peering at the stranger on the slippery rocks.

They could see the man quite clearly now. He was wearing black fisherman's oilskins, slick with sea spray, and a black sou'wester hat pulled low over his face. He did not seem to have heard Sherlock's barking over the sound of the waves and was facing away from them as he stared out to sea. The light in his hand was an old-style lantern, which he was swinging steadily back and forth. Far out to sea they could see a distant answering light blinking on and off.

"What did I tell you?" said Joe. "He's definitely a wrecker. You mark my words, there's going to be a shipwreck."

"That's ridiculous," said Lucy. "But, all the same, Sherlock really doesn't seem to like him. Maybe we should call the police."

"And tell them what?" panted Max. He was still struggling to gain his breath after his run along the beach. "That they should arrest this guy just because some stupid dog thinks he's suspicious?"

"Sherlock is not a stupid dog!" Charlie flared at him.

"He's smarter than most humans. Don't you ever say that about him, or I'll make you sorry."

"Cut it out," snapped Lucy. "We're supposed to be deciding what to do, not fighting amongst ourselves."

"Oh no!" cried Joe. "Look at Sherlock!"

While they had been arguing, Charlie had let go of Sherlock's collar, and the little dog had seized his chance. As soon as he was free, he leapt onto the granite rocks, making his way towards the mysterious stranger.

Sherlock scrambled over the rocks, scrabbling for purchase with his claws. He could smell that this man was up to no good. Humans never seemed to pay much attention to smells. They would walk around with their noses high in the air, missing all the interesting smells near the ground, and it never seemed to bother them. But Sherlock trusted his nose, and he knew that this man smelled of trouble.

And, of course, that meant that he, Sherlock, would have to do something about it. After all, a man like that might hurt his mistress, and Sherlock could never allow such a thing to happen.

"Sherlock, no!" screamed Charlie. "Come back here." Frantically, she clambered onto the wet rocks after him.

The children's yelling and Sherlock's barking cut across the noise of the waves, and the man on the rocks turned and noticed them for the first time. He lowered the lamp and glared at them. He was clearly not happy to see that he was being observed. His face was partially hidden in the shadows, but his mouth was clearly visible, the lips pulled back into a snarl, exposing a mouthful of crooked and missing teeth.

When the man saw Sherlock, he looked furious. He bent down and picked up a rock, raising it high above his head before hurling it at Sherlock. The rock missed Sherlock by a whisker, sailing over his head before bouncing away. As the rock fell into the sea, the man roared in frustration. It was a sound filled with so much anger and hatred that it chilled their blood. Even Charlie stopped chasing after Sherlock and stared at the man, wide-eyed in horror.

The roar did not stop Sherlock though. The little dog was now more determined than ever to protect his mistress. The man bent down to pick up a second rock just as Sherlock reached him. As the man raised the rock above his head, the little dog leapt and sank his teeth into the fleshy part of the man's calf.

The man let out a shriek of pain, and Sherlock writhed and twisted to avoid the blows the man aimed at him. Somewhere in the distance Sherlock heard Charlie screaming his name, and, in the same instant, the little dog felt a sharp pain as a hefty kick from the man caught him in the side.

The children heard the dull thump followed by a yelp before a tiny brown and white body tumbled over and over, down the slippery rocks and into the oily waters below.

Charlie screamed again. "Sherlock!" she cried. She turned to the others. "He's fallen into the water. He'll be killed by the rocks. Please, somebody help him!"

4

SHERLOCK IN TROUBLE

For a moment nobody moved. Max and Joe stared in shock as Charlie screamed for her dog. Then Lucy sprang into action, jumping down onto the sand next to Charlie, who was now beside herself with panic.

As the others followed, the seriousness of the problem was immediately apparent. Sherlock had taken a bad tumble into the sea. The waves were crashing heavily against the granite rocks, and a fierce undertow had already pulled the little dog several yards offshore. Sherlock was trying valiantly to swim against the current, but each time he came a little closer to the beach, the waves would drag him back out again. Lucy could see that he was beginning to tire.

"He'll be drowned!" cried Charlie. "I have to do something." She tore off her hooded sweatshirt and began to wade out towards Sherlock. Almost immediately a large wave knocked her over. It was only Lucy's quick action in grabbing hold of her arm that prevented Charlie from being dragged out too.

"You can't go out there, Charlie," she cried, gripping the girl's arm tightly. "The waves are too strong."

Charlie fought hard, trying to break Lucy's grip, but the older girl held on fast. They could see that Sherlock was getting weaker now. He was whining and struggling to keep his head above the water. Several times he was overwhelmed completely by the waves.

"Somebody throw him a rope!" cried Joe.

"We haven't got a rope, stupid!" yelled back Lucy. She was still holding onto Charlie, who was now sobbing desperately.

"We could form a human chain," shouted Max above the roar of the waves. "If we link up, one of us might be able to reach him and pull him back in."

"He's right," shouted Lucy. "Quick, everyone, join hands."

Moving quickly, they lined up on the shingle and grasped each other's wrists so that they formed a line. Charlie initially wanted to go at the front so she could reach Sherlock herself, but Lucy wouldn't let her. "It's too deep," she told Charlie. "And you're not as tall as me. Let me go first."

Even in her panicked state, Charlie saw the sense of what was being said and agreed. Holding onto Charlie's wrist, Lucy began to wade into the heaving black sea. She gasped for breath as the icy waters soaked through her thin tracksuit.

Charlie followed Lucy into the water and reached behind for Joe's hand as he waded in after her. Last of all came Max, the shortest. He clutched Joe's wrist with both hands, gritting his teeth and digging his heels into the shingle to stop them all being pulled out to sea.

Edging her way out carefully, Lucy began to wade forward, still clutching Charlie's wrist. She could feel the undertow pulling against her legs and threatening to drag her into the deep water. The sea was up to her chest now, and she felt dizzy from the cold, but she was only a few feet from Sherlock. The little dog was nearly exhausted, he was struggling to keep his head above water, and she could hear his pathetic whimpering as the waves washed over him.

Lucy stretched out her arm as far as she could, pulling against the others so that even Max was up to his waist in water. But Sherlock was still just out of reach. For a terrifying moment, she thought that he would sink beneath the water and be lost.

Then a huge wave surged forward, pushing the little dog towards her just enough for Lucy's fingers to hook beneath his collar. She dragged him closer as the big wave crashed down on them, washing them back towards the beach and drenching them all in freezing water.

There were several seconds of coughing and spluttering as they disentangled themselves from the sodden heap. Then, with a desperate sob, Charlie fell on Sherlock, pulling him close and covering him with kisses.

"Oh, Sherlock," she sobbed. "I'm so sorry. It's all my fault. I should have held onto you more tightly. I'm so sorry. I'm so sorry."

Sherlock himself looked shaken and a little wobbly. There was a small cut on his hindquarters, but otherwise he seemed unharmed. He whined a little and licked Charlie's face as she hugged him close, but very soon his tail began to wag again.

"Well," said Max as he watched the happy reunion, "I didn't expect to be doing *that* tonight." Then he remembered something, and his face fell. "Oh no! I forgot to take off my rucksack. My books will be ruined."

"I'm just glad Sherlock's okay," gasped Lucy. "For one terrible minute I thought we'd lost him."

Still clutching Sherlock, Charlie turned to face them. She looked pale and sick from the shock. "Thank you," she said weakly. "Thank you for saving Sherlock. He means the world to me. I don't know what I would have done if...if..."

"It's okay," said Lucy quickly. "I'm glad we could help. He certainly is a brave little chap, tackling that creepy guy all by himself."

"The wrecker!" cried Joe, looking around. "He's gone."

They looked up at the rocks and realised it was true. In the excitement of rescuing Sherlock, the mysterious stranger had disappeared. What was more there was no sign of the twinkling light out at sea either.

"I guess that means there won't be any shipwrecks tonight," said Max. "Chalk one up to the good guys."

At that moment it began to rain in fat, freezing pellets

that stung their faces and reminded them of just how cold
they all were. "I'm freezing," said Max suddenly. His teeth
were chattering so hard that he could barely get the
words out.

"Me too," said Lucy. She got up and slapped her arms
vigorously, trying to warm herself, but it was of little use.
The bitter sea and the heavy rain had driven the cold deep
into their bones, and they were all shivering violently now.
Lucy knew from her training how dangerous being exposed
to the cold could be and how quickly it could make a person
very sick indeed. "We have to get warm," she said. "And
quickly, or we could develop hypothermia out here."

"Get warm how?" said Max. "We can't exactly rub two
sticks together, can we?"

Charlie stood and picked Sherlock up in her arms. "I'll
have to take him home," she said. "He's shivering, and he'll
get a chill if I don't get him dry soon."

"It's a long way back to town," said Lucy, looking along
the beach. "We'll all be frozen solid by the time we get
there."

"I know a place we can go," said Joe suddenly. "It's
perfect. And it's really close by."

Max grunted. "This isn't some made-up place, is it? Like
those imaginary friends of yours?"

"No, honestly," said Joe. "I can take you there now."

Lucy frowned at Joe. "This had better be true, Joe," she
said sternly. "I'm serious. We need to get warm quickly."

"Well, come on then," said Joe. "There's no time to lose."

Before any of them could ask another question, Joe
jumped to his feet and started back down the beach in a
stiff-limbed trot. "Hurry up," he yelled back over his shoulder. "Stop dawdling, you lot."

Lucy shrugged. "Well, I suppose we'd better follow him," she said. "At least it's in the right direction."

Charlie scowled. "If he's lying about this, I'm going to kill him with my bare hands."

"If he's lying," said Max, "I'll hold him down while you do it."

5

THE BEST PLACE IN THE WORLD

Joe led them back in the direction of the town. Nobody spoke as they struggled across the damp sand in a long line. The sea wind cut through their wet clothes, making them feel stiff and slow. Lucy was worried. She knew how important it was to keep warm and how quickly a person could become very ill if they were exposed to the cold and wet for too long.

As though she were reading her thoughts, Charlie called out from the back of the group, "How much further? I'm worried about Sherlock. He's shivering like anything."

"Don't worry, we're here," said Joe. He brought them to a halt at the place where the beach huts began.

The last beach hut in the row was painted in summer sea colours of blue and turquoise. It had two wooden steps and white wooden handrails. Joe crouched, reached beneath a plank, and retrieved something from underneath. It was a key.

"Got it!" he said triumphantly. "I just hope the lock hasn't rusted up."

The others stared in amazement at the beautiful little beach hut. "Is this really yours?" said Lucy.

"Yeah." Joe nodded. "My dad bought it when he was trying to persuade my mum that we should move to Southwold."

"He *bought* it?" said Max. "I asked my mum and dad if we could hire a beach hut for a day last summer, but they said they cost far too much money."

Joe shrugged. "I don't know how much Dad paid for it, but I remember him telling his friends that he'd 'paid an arm and a leg for a glorified shed'."

Lucy ran a hand along the white-painted rails. "Well, I think it's beautiful," she said. "Your family must spend all their time here when the weather's nice."

Joe made a face and looked down at his shoes. "We only came the once," he said. "Mum hated it. She said the sand got everywhere, and it wasn't 'exclusive' enough. I don't know what that means, but I remember they had a big row about it, and we had to leave early. After that, Dad locked it up and said he was going to sell it the next day. But then he went away on business, and I think he forgot all about it."

Max and Lucy stared at Joe. Neither of them could imagine their families owning something as wonderful as their own beach hut, let alone forgetting all about it.

Their thoughts were interrupted by Charlie. "If you're all done admiring the beach hut," she said, "I need to get Sherlock inside. Now!"

Joe jiggled the key in the lock while the others looked on. The lock was crusted with salt, and it took some time to work it free, but suddenly the door swung open. Joe disappeared inside, and the others squeezed through the entrance after him. Joe scrabbled around in the dark until he found a box of matches and lit a small lamp standing in the corner.

A warm yellow glow filled the little cabin, illuminating a tidy space with faded blue rugs laid on the wood floor. There was a low counter along one wall and wide bench seats with colourful throws and fat squashy cushions.

"Oh my!" said Lucy. "I never saw a beach hut as lovely as this one before."

"You could live in here," said Max.

Joe struck another match and crouched down beside the heater. There was a low 'whoomph', and a yellow flame sprang up. The children gathered around it with outstretched hands, sighing with pleasure as the warm glow seeped into their fingers.

"There are towels in here," said Joe, opening a cupboard. "And some bathrobes too. Mum sent off for them from a shop in London, but we never used them."

Charlie immediately grabbed a thick towel and sat down in front of the fire to dry Sherlock. The little dog shivered as she worked, rubbing him vigorously to get some warmth back into his muscles.

Max grabbed another towel and wrapped it around himself. The towel was dry and fluffy and covered him down to his feet. Gratefully he peeled off his wet socks and jeans and spread them out on the floor near to the fire. Then he took off his tie and draped it carefully over the fire, smoothing out the damp wrinkles carefully as he did so.

Lucy had wrapped herself in a bathrobe and was wringing out her wet tracksuit at the door. "This is the best place in the world."

Joe beamed and puffed out his chest as his new friends made themselves comfortable. "Er, how about a drink?" he said. "I can fix us something hot." There was a camping stove on the counter with a shiny new kettle on top. Joe reached up and took down some tins from a shelf, prising off the lids to inspect their contents. "There's some hot chocolate in here," he said. "And bottled water that I can boil in the kettle."

"Hot chocolate would be the best thing ever right now," said Max. Still wrapped in his towel, he had installed himself into the corner of the hut and was making himself comfortable amongst the cushions. "I don't suppose you've got anything to eat in there, have you?"

Joe opened another cupboard and poked around inside. "There's some shortbread biscuits in here," he said. "They haven't been opened, so they should still be alright."

At the mention of biscuits, Sherlock gave a loud bark and jumped up from Charlie's lap, with his tail wagging and his eyes fixed firmly on the packet. Next to sausages, biscuits were absolutely Sherlock's favourite thing.

The children laughed at the sudden interruption. "Well, he seems to be back to his old self," said Lucy. She noticed Charlie's worried expression and laid a hand on her shoulder. "Don't worry about him," she said. "I'm sure he'll be absolutely fine."

"And I'm sure he'd like one of these," said Joe, taking a biscuit from the packet. Then he paused and glanced nervously at Charlie. "If...you'd like to give him one, that is." He held out the packet towards her.

Charlie looked at the packet and then at Joe. "It's okay," she said. "You can feed him a biscuit if you want to."

Joe beamed even wider and bent down to offer the biscuit to Sherlock, who took it gently from Joe's hand, then ate it noisily on the rug, much to everyone's amusement. At that moment the kettle warbled to life, and, in no time, Joe was handing around steaming mugs of hot chocolate and shortbread. The biscuits were a little soggy, and the hot chocolate was quite lumpy, but the children agreed that they were the best things they'd had to eat and drink all year.

"I could happily sleep in here," said Max from his corner. "It's more comfortable than my bed. Toby Watts would never think of looking for me in here."

"If my family had a place as nice as this," said Lucy, snuggling down in the opposite corner, "I think I'd come here every day. If my dad would let me have the time off from training, that is," she added wistfully.

"I came here by myself once or twice," said Joe. "But having nice things isn't much fun if you don't have friends to share them with."

"So, what about you, Charlie?" said Lucy, noticing that the girl had become very quiet. "Wouldn't you like a place like this to hang out?"

Charlie shrugged. "It's okay, I guess," she said without

looking at Lucy. "But most of the time, me and Sherlock are just out on our own." She held up her binoculars. "We go bird spotting in the dunes, so a place like this would be wasted on the two of us. I think we can manage fine without it."

Lucy frowned. She found the fierce little girl very strange indeed and would have liked to know more about her, but Charlie clearly wasn't the talking kind.

But if Charlie was quiet, then Sherlock was the opposite. The little dog was having the time of his life amongst the children. He ate three more biscuits, including one he managed to sneak out of the packet when no one was looking. Then he barked and rolled over and allowed his tummy to be tickled as the children took turns petting him.

Sherlock was very glad that his mistress had decided to be friends with these children, particularly the tall girl who had pulled him out of the water. They were definitely good people, he decided as he curled up for a sleep in front of the fire.

Satisfied that his guests were well provided for, Joe settled himself on the couch between Lucy and Max with his cocoa. "So," he began, "what are we going to do about our ghostly wrecker?"

Max snorted scornfully. "There's no such thing as ghosts," he said. "Or wreckers either for that matter."

"Well, whoever he was," said Lucy, "he was behaving very suspiciously. Maybe we should tell the police what we saw?"

"We don't have any evidence," said Joe. "The police would probably just tell us off for mucking around on the sea wall."

"Besides," said Max, "he didn't actually do anything

except stand around with a light in his hand. There's no crime against that."

"He *did* hurt Sherlock," said Charlie, her grey eyes flashing. "And I'll never forgive him for that. Sherlock could have been..." She paused. "He could have..." She stopped speaking altogether and bit her lip as though the next words were too awful to say.

Hearing his name mentioned, Sherlock was suddenly awake. He jumped up and licked Charlie's face. The girl was taken by surprise, and the change in her expression was instantaneous. She laughed. "Cut it out, Sherlock. Your tongue's all covered in biscuit crumbs."

The others laughed too, and pretty soon Sherlock was jumping up on the cushions again and taking it in turns to lick their faces so that it made them all giggle. "Thank you," said Charlie suddenly, looking around at the others in turn. "Thank you all for helping me to save Sherlock. I don't know what I would have done if you hadn't been there."

Max and Joe looked bashful and shrugged as though wading into the sea in the middle of winter had been nothing at all. Lucy smiled. "You're welcome," she said.

"And I'm sorry I was so horrible to you earlier," said Charlie to Joe. "It's just that Sherlock and me are on our own so much that we've never really trusted anyone else before."

Joe went all pink and pushed his floppy hair out of his eyes, the way he did when he was feeling embarrassed. "That's okay," he said. "I wish my mum would let me have a dog, but she says they jump all over the furniture. I think Sherlock's the best dog in the world."

Charlie beamed when Joe said this, and it was like the sun coming out from behind a cloud. "Yes, he is!" she said. "And you're welcome to feed him or pet him any time you want to. All of you are." She stood up suddenly and placed her mug on the counter. "Thanks for the chocolate. But me and Sherlock have to go. It's getting late."

"Oh no, is that the time?" Max had pulled his phone from the waterproof pouch inside his rucksack and was staring at it in horror. "My folks will be furious. I still have homework to do."

Joe laughed. "I never usually bother with my homework, and Mum never asks."

"My mum *always* asks," said Max as he retrieved his tie from on top of the fire. "And she regards not doing your homework as a hanging offence."

Lucy looked at her fitness watch and made a face. "I've got to get back too," she said. "My dad thinks I'm still out running."

A look of dismay crossed Joe's face. "Wait, don't all go just yet," he said. "We were just getting to know each other. Stick around. I'll make some more hot chocolate."

But the others were already on their feet, pulling on damp jeans and socks and collecting their things. Joe's party seemed to be over.

"At least let's agree to meet up again," he said. "We could try to find out some more information about the wrecker."

"And how exactly are we going to do that?" said Max, stuffing a pulpy exercise book back into his bag. "Just ask random people in the street?"

"There's a museum in town," said Joe. "I had to go there when we did a school project on the lighthouse. They might be able to tell us something about wreckers. Come on, it'll be fun to hang out together. Shall we say tomorrow at ten o'clock?"

There was a desperate look in his eyes that made Lucy feel sorry for Joe. "I'm not sure," she said. "My dad doesn't much like me hanging around with other kids. He thinks it's bad for my training."

"Hanging around with other kids is usually bad for my health," said Max. "Particularly when they're called Toby Watts. Besides, Saturday morning is when I help out in the shop."

Charlie shrugged and looked non-committal. "I don't know," she said. "Me and Sherlock were going to look for a kestrels' nest tomorrow. We're usually pretty busy at weekends, so I guess not." And before anyone could say anything more, she had opened the door and slipped out into the night, closely followed by Sherlock.

But Joe was not ready to give up just yet. "Promise me you'll both come?" he said to Lucy and Max.

Max shrugged. "Can't promise anything," he said. "But if I don't see you, good luck with catching the wrecker." He stood in the open doorway. "Coming, Luce?"

Lucy felt pained by the look on Joe's face, and she gave him a sympathetic smile. "I can't promise anything either," she said. "But we will try. Thanks again for the hot chocolate." She paused and looked around the cabin. "This really is the best place in the world."

And with that, she and Max left, leaving Joe to stare at the door. After a while he let out a sigh and began to collect up the mugs. *Maybe they will come tomorrow*, he thought to himself. It would be nice to have friends to do things with on a Saturday. But deep down he didn't hold out much hope.

6

CAPTAIN TOM

The next morning Joe hurried through the High Street on his way to the museum, wearing an anxious look. What if they didn't come? What if his new friends decided to stay home or hang out with their other friends, or just go for a walk on their own with the dog? What if Joe was on his own again? After the fun he'd had the previous night, he didn't think he could bear to spend the day all by himself.

His mother had arrived home late, and she was still in bed when he let himself out of the house and headed down the hill towards town. The day was fresh and bright after the miserable weather of the night before. Joe jogged past shopkeepers laying out fruit and veg or placing freshly baked loaves in their shop windows. He didn't stop to speak to anyone or even pause to glance up at the towering whitewashed walls of the great lighthouse in the centre of town. He didn't stop running until he reached the squat little museum at the end of Victoria Street, with its curly-topped roof that always reminded him of the gingerbread house from the fairy tales.

The clock on St Edmunds Church read ten minutes to ten. He waited patiently, watching the Saturday morning shoppers heading into town, and looking up and down the street for any sign of his friends. But by the time the clock struck quarter past the hour, his face had fallen. They weren't coming.

With a heavy heart he turned away from the museum and had just started the long walk home when there was a shout from behind him. "Hey, Joe. Wait up."

He turned to see Lucy pounding along the pavement towards him in a yellow tracksuit.

"Hi!" he called back. "You actually came!"

"Don't sound so surprised," she said, coming to a halt beside him. "Sorry I'm a bit late. Dad was furious that I was out so long last night. I had to wait until he went to work before I could get out again." She looked around. "Where are the others?"

Joe shrugged. "Couldn't make it, I guess," he said. "But I'm glad you're here, at least. Shall we go in?"

They turned towards the museum entrance and were about to go inside when another shout echoed down the street. "Hey, losers! Wait for me!"

They turned to see the extraordinary sight of Max riding on a sleek-looking skateboard. The board glided noiselessly along the street towards them without any apparent effort on Max's part, coming to a smooth stop right outside the museum.

"What *is* that thing?" said Lucy.

"Battery-operated skateboard," said Max. "I made it myself out of spare parts from the shop."

Lucy smiled. She knew that Max's parents ran a computer shop and that Max was extremely clever at making all kinds of gadgets in his bedroom. The skateboard was a first, though.

Joe looked at it with envious eyes. "That's the coolest thing I ever saw."

"Thanks," said Max, picking up the machine and stowing it under his arm. "Believe me, this is how everyone will travel in the future. So, have you found out anything about your 'ghost wrecker' yet?"

"We were just about to go in," said Lucy.

Joe took one last look along the street. "I was hoping Charlie and Sherlock might come too," he said. "But I guess they went bird spotting instead."

The trio entered the front door and stood for a moment, eyes wide with amazement. The museum was tiny but crammed full of glass cases, prints and photographs, and strange contraptions from bygone days. A crusty-looking gentleman with white whiskers and a naval cap gave them a nod from his chair in the corner, then went back to his newspaper.

They began to explore the contents of the museum, calling out to each other with delight when they found something new. A glass case along one wall was filled with bones, fossils and even mammoths' teeth that had been dug up locally. Others held moths, butterflies, stuffed birds and a scale model of a wooden sailing ship, complete with cloth sails.

There was a pair of giant wooden oars hanging on the walls that were said to belong to a Viking longship, and cannonballs that had actually been fired in a sea battle. Joe was fascinated by a display of guns and swords, and Lucy liked looking at the old children's toys fashioned out of painted wood and tin. Max was particularly taken with the medicine chest that had a special compartment for poisons.

But, however hard they looked, they could find no mention of wreckers or ghosts or anything that might explain the mysterious stranger they had seen the night before. "I've had enough of this," said Max after an hour of looking. "There's nothing that can help us in here, and I need some sunlight. It's so dark and musty in this place."

With heavy hearts they filed out of the museum and back onto the pavement, blinking in the winter sunlight. Standing outside, they found a familiar small figure with plaited hair and a small dog sitting by her side.

Sherlock barked with delight at seeing the other children again. He jumped up and licked their hands and scampered around their feet until Charlie scolded him, and he sat down with a shame-faced expression.

Joe laughed. "Charlie!" he said. "I knew you'd come."

The girl shrugged. "I didn't think they'd let Sherlock in the museum, so we waited until you were finished," she said. "So how did you all get on?"

"We didn't find very much," said Joe gloomily. "I mean, there's loads of interesting stuff in there. But we couldn't find anything about ghosts."

"So it's ghosts you're looking for, is it, young man?" said a voice from behind them.

They turned to see the crusty old gentleman they had seen inside the museum. He wore a thick navy pea-jacket, buttoned up to the top, and a blue and white spotted scarf around his neck. His naval cap was pushed back on his head, and he was watching them with sparkling blue eyes. He looked like something that had stepped out of a book about ancient seafarers.

Joe blinked. "Er, y-yes," he stammered. "We were looking for information about local ghosts."

"It's for a school project," added Lucy quickly.

"Not that we believe in ghosts ourselves, you understand," said Max.

The old man nodded sagely. "Aye, there's plenty around here as don't believe in ghosts," he said. "All I know is..." He leaned towards them and lowered his voice to a dramatic whisper. "It makes little difference to the ghosts whether you believes in 'em or not."

The children stared at him. Lucy was the first to speak. "Didn't we see you inside the museum?"

The old man nodded. "That you did," he said. "Thomas Crofford's the name, though round here most people call me Cap'n Tom." He pointed to where the lantern panes of the lighthouse were visible at the end of the street above the other buildings. "I was the lighthouse keeper there for nigh on thirty years. But nowadays I just help out in the museum when I can. There's not much I don't know about Southwold's ghostly past. Not that you believe in that sort of thing, of course," he added with a wink at Max.

"I believe in them," said Joe quickly. "So, are you saying that there really are actual ghosts, right here in Southwold?"

"Bless my soul, I reckon there's more ghosts than there are people in these old buildings," he said with a laugh. "I tell you what, I've just stepped out for a quick pipe and a sit down on yonder benches." He nodded towards the churchyard across the street. "If you've got a minute or two to spare, I'll see if I can help you out with your school project."

Without waiting for an answer, Captain Tom strode across the street towards a bench that overlooked the gravestones in the churchyard. The children looked at one another and then followed. Max noted that Captain Tom walked with a strange rolling gait, like a man who has spent a lifetime walking on an unsteady ship's deck. Yet he still walked fast enough that the children had to run to keep up with him.

The old man settled on the bench as the children gathered around him. He produced a long pipe from his pocket, and they waited expectantly as he tamped down a thick plug of sweet-smelling tobacco with his thumb.

"Smoking's a dirty habit," said Charlie.

Lucy frowned at her. Really, she thought, this girl could be extremely rude at times.

Captain Tom looked up and narrowed his eyes at Charlie. "It most certainly is, young lady," he said sternly. He pointed at her with the stem of his pipe. "And that is why I'm planning to give it up on my hundredth birthday. But until then..." He struck a match and sucked the pipe to life before blowing out a plume of blue smoke. "A pipe smoker I shall be."

Charlie looked a bit sheepish, and Lucy had to stifle a grin. Captain Tom settled back on the bench. "So, what is it you'd like to know about the ghosts in this town?"

They looked at each other nervously. Joe licked his lips. Up until now he had been certain that the strange figure they had seen on the beach had been a wrecker or a ghost, or both. But speaking about it in front of an adult made him feel suddenly foolish. "We...heard a story," he said slowly. "Someone we know told us they saw a man carrying a lamp down by the sea wall. They said he was really creepy looking and that he was signalling to a boat out at sea. We...I mean *they* thought he might be a wrecker."

"Or a ghost," added Max.

"Or the ghost of a wrecker," said Joe.

Captain Tom's brow furrowed. He took the pipe from his mouth and blew a perfect smoke ring, waiting until it had drifted away before he spoke again. "Well," he said after a long wait, "I've not heard many stories about wreckers in these parts. Wrong sort of coastline around here, see. But I've heard a lot of ghost stories in my time, and I reckon your friends might have seen the Spectre of Southwold Sands."

"A spectre!" gasped Max.

"Here in Southwold?" gasped Joe.

"Is that a real thing?" said Lucy.

Captain Tom shrugged. "Real enough to them what's seen him," he said. "They say he's the departed soul of a fisherman who lived in these parts nigh on two hundred years ago. Legend has it that one night he was lost at sea in a dreadful storm and feared he would surely drown. He was so afraid that he prayed to the spirits of the sea to deliver him home safe. It just so happened that, at that very moment, a mermaid was passing by and heard his prayer. She appeared from the waves beside his boat and offered to guide the fisherman to safety, but only if he would marry her and make her into a human bride."

"A mermaid?" said Lucy, her eyes wide. "So, what did he do?"

"What could he do?" said the old man. "The fisherman agreed to the deal, and he let the mermaid take him back to the harbour and to safety. But fear is a strange thing. The moment a man feels safe again, he forgets all about it. As soon as he was safely back on dry land, he laughed at the mermaid and told her he wouldn't marry her because he was due to be wed to his childhood sweetheart. The mermaid was furious. She cursed him and swore that if he or any of his loved ones ever went to sea again, that she would claim them for her own."

"Somehow, I'm guessing this didn't end well," said Max.

Captain Tom's eyebrows knitted together in a thick white hedge. "It did not," he said gravely. "The fisherman was worried enough about the mermaid's curse that he gave up fishing altogether, and he forbade any of his family from ever going to sea."

There was a pause while Captain Tom tapped the embers from his pipe, and the children waited impatiently. "A year passed, and the fisherman forgot all about the mermaid as he made preparations to marry his sweetheart. But, on the very day of their wedding, his bride-to-be decided to surprise her husband by catching a fresh crab for their wedding supper. She went down to the boatyard and took out his old fishing boat, forgetting all about her promise to stay away from the sea."

The children were hanging on the captain's every word. "What happened to her?" asked Joe in a whisper.

"As soon as she was out at sea," continued Captain Tom, "a terrible storm blew in from the north. The storm was so fierce, it was like something from hell itself. It smashed the little boat and drowned the poor girl in an instant. When the fisherman found out what had happened, he knew it was the work of the mermaid, and that he was to blame for the death of his bride. The poor man was so distraught that he threw himself into the sea and was drowned also. The mermaid's revenge was complete."

"That's terrible," said Lucy.

Captain Tom nodded. "Terrible it might have been," he said. "But he should have known better than to cross a sea spirit. They say it's his ghost that still walks the sands, with a lantern in his hand, looking for his lost bride. They also say that it's an ill omen for anyone who sees him."

"An 'ill omen'?" said Joe. "What's one of those?"

"It means that something bad is going to happen," said Captain Tom in a dark voice.

"You don't really believe those old tales, do you?" asked

Charlie. "All that stuff about mermaids and curses and ghosts. It's not real."

"An old tale it might be," said Captain Tom, "but there's plenty around here that take it seriously enough." He stood up and slipped his pipe back into his pocket. "Now, if you'll all excuse me, I need to be getting back to my duties. But if I were you," he added, "I'd warn your friends to stay away from the sea wall on a winter's night. After all, you never know when you might see *the Spectre*."

7

THE HARBOURMASTER

Nobody spoke as they watched the old man disappear back inside the museum. Joe shivered. "Brr, that tale's given me the creeps. Do you believe all that stuff about the mermaid's curse? Is something really bad going to happen to us just because we saw the fisherman?"

"You idiot," snapped Charlie. "He was just pulling your leg. There's no curse, and there's no ghostly fisherman either. He was just trying to frighten us to make us stay off the sea wall."

"Still, it was a pretty good story," said Max. He felt suddenly chilly and rubbed his arms to keep warm. Even though he didn't believe in ghosts, he had to admit that the old man's tale had made the hairs on the back of his neck stand up.

"Well, after all that spookiness, I think we need something to take our minds off things," said Lucy. "How about we all go for an ice cream? My treat."

"An ice cream!" said Max. "Are you nuts? It's the middle of winter."

"So what?" asked Lucy, grinning. "I love ice cream at any time of year. I hardly ever get to eat sweets with all my training, but I'll always make an exception for ice cream."

"Nowhere sells ice cream at this time of year," said Joe.

"Not true," said Lucy. "There's a kiosk at the end of the harbour where they sell ice creams all year round. It's where I go for my secret supplies."

"The harbour's miles away," complained Max.

"It's less than a mile along the sand dunes," said Charlie. "Me and Sherlock walk it a lot. And besides, I like ice cream too." She caught Lucy's eye and gave her the smallest of smiles.

At the mention of the word 'walk', Sherlock raised his head and barked agreement. On Saturday mornings, he and his mistress always went for long walks, and he could not understand why they had spent so long in one place today. Museums were definitely not the sort of thing that interested dogs.

"That settles it, then," said Lucy. "Come on, Max. The walk'll do you good."

They ignored Max's groans of protest and headed off through the town, with Sherlock leading the way, hoovering the pavement for smells as they went. They cut through an alley to Gun Hill, passing the row of old brass cannons that faced out to sea, and heading down onto the beach where the sand dunes began.

The sky was blue, and the sun was clear and bright, and a fresh breeze blew the waves into foam-topped breakers. "I can't believe it's such a lovely day," said Lucy. "Especially after all the foul weather we had last night."

"Sherlock and I love coming here in winter," said Charlie. "Dogs aren't allowed on the beach in the summer, so it's the best time of year for us."

Sherlock was already scampering across the dunes, his doggy ears inside out in the wind. He kept his nose close to the ground for the scent of seagulls. Sherlock regarded seagulls as the finest sport a dog could get. He would chase them whenever he got the opportunity, and Charlie would get angry and try to stop him whenever he did. Seagulls were about the only thing that Sherlock and Charlie ever disagreed on.

The walk along the sand dunes was bright and refreshing, even though Max complained continuously that his electric skateboard didn't work on the sand and that it was too heavy to be carrying all this way. "I mean, what is the point," he said for the tenth time, "of having one of the most advanced forms of transport known to man if you have to pick it up and stuff it under your arm?"

"Stop moaning," said Lucy. "We're nearly there."

At the southern end of the dunes, they passed the summer campsites, now empty and deserted, and reached the point where the River Blyth met the coastline. At the mouth of the harbour, an old jetty stuck out into the sea like a concrete and steel finger, and the wind howled across the empty car park. But just as Lucy had predicted, a blue-painted kiosk was open for business, offering teas, coffees, milkshakes, scones and...*ice creams.*

Lucy ran over to the kiosk and returned a few moments later with four vanilla cones, all sprouting chocolate flakes. "You are nuts, Lucy Yeung," said Max. "It's the middle of December."

"I'll eat yours if you don't want it." Joe laughed; he had already taken a huge mouthful.

"Don't worry," said Max with a grin. "I'll force it down. Thanks, Luce."

As well as the ice creams, Lucy had also bought a packet

of dog biscuits for Sherlock, which she handed to Charlie. "Thank you," said Charlie as she took the packet. "It's very good of you to think of Sherlock too."

Lucy shrugged. "Of course," she said. "He's one of the gang too."

"So we're a gang now?" said Joe, brightening. "We're an actual gang?"

Max shrugged. "I guess so," he said. "But if anyone makes me walk much further today, I'm putting in for a transfer."

For a while, nobody spoke as they strolled along the bank, licking their ice creams. They passed shuttered booths that offered boat trips to the tourists in summer, fishermen's huts with corrugated tin roofs, rusty winches, and empty oil drums collecting rainwater.

A line of grey gulls stood expectantly on the wooden pilings where the fishing vessels tied up, hoping for a dropped fish. Sherlock gave them a sideways glance but quickly returned his attention to the packet of dog biscuits in Charlie's hand. The seagulls could wait for now.

The three of them sat on some wooden railings over-looking a concrete slipway while they finished their cones. Charlie broke the biscuits into smaller pieces and handed them around so they could take turns feeding Sherlock, an arrangement that suited Sherlock very well.

Their perch gave them a view across the river to Walber-swick and the flat marshlands on the other side, criss-crossed with hedgerows, long grasses and purple-headed rushes. The harbour itself was bleak and deserted. Many of the larger boats had been taken out of the water for the winter and had been raised up on wooden blocks with black tarpaulins lashed tightly across their upper decks.

"Do you suppose boats feel sad when they can't be in the

water?" asked Joe, crunching his ice-cream cone. "I think it would make me sad if I couldn't do the thing I was made to do."

Charlie frowned. "Do you always say the first thing that comes into your head?" she said. "Regardless of how stupid it sounds?"

"Pretty much," said Joe, finishing the remains of his ice cream in a single bite. "My school report said I always spend too much time daydreaming."

Max was looking along the harbour front at a spot where a scruffy man was loading boxes into a large rubber dinghy. A short distance away, a motorbike had pulled up close to the quayside. As soon as the scruffy man saw the motorbike, he stopped what he was doing and scowled. The rider dismounted and approached the dinghy, and the two immediately began having a heated conversation.

"What do you suppose is going on over there?" said Max. "It looks like those two are pretty annoyed with each other."

The children could not hear clearly what was being said, but the odd words reached them above the noise of the wind. "Where were...last night...waiting?" growled the scruffy man. He jabbed an accusing finger at the motorcyclist when he spoke. "You were supposed to be...Can't afford any more of your mess-ups..."

The motorcyclist also seemed to be quite agitated. He was still wearing his helmet, so they could not hear what he was saying clearly, but he shrugged his shoulders and held out his hands, palms upwards in an 'it's not my fault' sort of gesture.

The scruffy man was beginning to get really angry now. He shouted something more loudly, but Sherlock chose that moment to begin barking, and the words were lost. The instant the little dog had seen the two men, his ears had gone back and he had begun to growl. Now he was barking like a dog twice his size.

"Be quiet, Sherlock," hissed Charlie. "We're trying to hear." But even though Charlie grabbed him firmly by the collar, Sherlock would not stop barking, and they could hear no more of what was being said.

Worse still, the noise had attracted the attention of the two men, who were now staring in their direction. The scruffy man scowled at the children and then beckoned the motorcyclist into a nearby boat shed and out of sight.

"They looked pretty suspicious if you ask me," said Joe.

"You think everyone's suspicious," said Lucy.

"Well, Sherlock certainly didn't like either of them," said Charlie. "And he's *always* a good judge of character."

"I think Sherlock might be right," said Max thoughtfully. "Did you notice the man on the motorcycle had a piece torn out of his jeans in exactly the spot where Sherlock bit Joe's ghost last night?"

The others stared at Max in amazement. "I didn't notice that," said Lucy. "How on earth did you manage to see something so tiny?"

Max smirked. "I always like to think of myself as a details man."

"You don't think that man's a ghost, do you?" asked Joe. "He looked real enough to me."

"Don't be ridiculous," said Max. "Of course he's not a ghost. But I think he might have been pretending to be one last night. And Sherlock obviously thinks so too."

"But why would anyone stand on a beach and pretend to be a ghost?" asked Charlie. "That makes no sense at all."

"Unless he was up to no good," said Joe. "Perhaps he'd also heard the story of the fisherman and the mermaid, and he thought it would be a good way to scare people away. Maybe he really is a wrecker after all?"

"Captain Tom said there were no wreckers in these parts," said Lucy. "It must be something else."

"But what?" said Joe.

Before anyone could offer an idea about what the man had been doing, they were interrupted by a thin, nasally voice coming from behind them. "And what exactly are you four up to?"

The children all jumped with surprise. They had been so intent on watching the two men that they had not noticed someone approaching them from behind. They turned around to see a pinched-looking man wearing a naval uniform. His peaked white cap was pulled so low that he had to peer down his nose to see them properly.

The man's uniform might once have been impressive. It had a double-breasted jacket and large buttons that looked like chocolate coins covered in gold foil. But the jacket was several sizes too large for him, and the trousers were spotted with grease. It looked like something he had bought in a second-hand store.

"Who are you?" said Max.

"Who am I?" repeated the man incredulously, as though everyone ought to know who he was. He leaned in closer. "I'll tell you who I am, young man," he said, giving Max a whiff of his eggy breath. "I'll have you know that I am none other than the Queen's Harbourmaster. Creech is the name. Walter Creech."

Mr Creech's beady rat eyes roamed over the children as he curled his lip. Joe noticed that he had a postage-stamp-sized patch of hair beneath his nose that twitched every time he talked. "I'll have you know that I have the power to arrest miscreants within this vicinity."

"Mis-what?" said Joe with a frown.

"It means troublemakers," said Mr Creech, baring his yellow teeth as he spoke. "Like you lot."

"But we haven't done anything," said Lucy. "We just came here to eat our ice creams."

"Don't give me that!" snapped Mr Creech. "I saw you eyeing up those boat sheds. You've come here to steal something, I bet. I'm going to call your parents." He pulled out a clipboard from behind his back. "Right then, names and addresses, please."

Lucy was incensed. "Now look here!" She drew herself up to her full height, which was almost as tall as Mr Creech, and looked him straight in the eye. "We don't have to give you our names and addresses," she said. "We've as much right to be here as anyone else."

"Hang on a minute," said Mr Creech, looking past Lucy. He had caught sight of Charlie standing at the back of the group. "I know you! You're the one who owns that vicious little dog."

Sherlock could not understand anything that was being said, but he didn't like Mr Creech's tone one little bit. He bared his teeth at the harbourmaster and barked. The effect on Mr Creech was immediate.

"Oh my gawd! There he is!" he cried. His eyes widened with fear, and he jumped behind Lucy, holding out his clipboard in front of him like a shield. "Keep that beast away from me. He bit my leg last summer. He's vicious, he is."

Charlie grabbed Sherlock's collar and scowled at Mr Creech. "He's not vicious," she said. "He only bit you because you threw cold water over him. Besides, he didn't even break the skin."

Mr Creech scowled. "Don't think I don't know who you are, young lady," he said. "You're that Charlotte Wells with the crazy mother who lets you run wild. A half-wild kid with a half-wild dog, that's what you are. I've a good mind to call the police and have that dog put down."

"No!" Charlie gasped in horror. She shrank back from Mr Creech, and her face turned as pale as death. "You can't do that!" she cried. "Sherlock's done you no harm. He, he…"

Charlie was suddenly lost for words. Her eyes filled with tears of rage, and she crouched down and pulled Sherlock closer to her. "You can't take him away. You just can't!" Hot tears spilled down her cheeks.

Max, Lucy and Joe looked on helplessly at the unhappy Charlie. Mr Creech looked very pleased with himself, and a nasty smile had spread across his face. Then Max stepped forward and tapped him on the shoulder.

"As I understand it, Mr Creech," he said, "the harbourmaster is responsible for the safety of all vessels whilst they are in the harbour. Isn't that true?"

Mr Creech looked down his nose at Max. The postage-stamp moustache twitched in an irritated fashion. "More or less," he said cautiously.

"Well," said Max, "it looks to me like there's a boat over there with a loose tarpaulin flapping in the breeze. That could cause a nasty accident if someone doesn't do something about it."

The tiny moustache twitched back and forth like a dancing caterpillar under Mr Creech's nose. "Now look here, you little squirt," he began.

"And furthermore," said Max, pointing to a row of oil tanks beside a boat shed, "one of those oil tanks is dripping fuel oil, which constitutes an environmental and a fire hazard." Max adopted a pained expression. "I'd hate to have to tell the authorities that the harbourmaster isn't doing his job properly."

"What?" Mr Creech looked startled. His eyes darted from the loose tarpaulin to the dripping oil tank and back again. "Well...I-I was just about to do something about those things," he stammered. "But I got distracted by you lot." He began to back away, holding out the clipboard in front of him as he went. "Anyway, I don't have time to stand here talking to kids all day. I've got work to do. Just mind you don't get up to any more mischief."

He continued to back away until he was sure he was a safe distance from Sherlock. Then, with as much dignity as he could muster, he straightened his jacket and marched away stiffly. Lucy, Joe and Charlie watched him go with open mouths.

"Max," gasped Lucy when he had gone, "that was amazing!"

Max shrugged in an 'it was nothing' sort of way. "My dad says you should always stand up to bullies," he said. Then he sighed. "I only wish I could get it to work on Toby Watts and his idiot mates. But the last time I tried something like that on them, they made me eat sand."

"Well, I think you did great," said Joe admiringly. "Did you see the way Creech went slinking off with his tail between his legs?"

"Thank you, Max," said Charlie quietly. She still looked pale and scared, but she managed a small smile. "I'd die if someone tried to take Sherlock away from me."

"Well, nobody's going to do that," said Lucy. "At least not while we're your friends. We can fight off harbourmasters and ghosts alike."

"Speaking of our ghost," said Max, "it looks like he's on the move."

While they had been dealing with Mr Creech, the two men had emerged from the boat shed. The motorcyclist quickly mounted his motorbike and roared away in a cloud of blue smoke. The scruffy man scowled at them from a distance and then walked to his dinghy. In just a few moments he had started the outboard engine and was steering away from the dockside. He glared at them from under dark eyebrows as the dinghy chugged past them and out towards the open sea.

"Where's he going in such a tiny boat?" said Lucy. "It's not big enough to get very far."

"My guess is he's heading for that yacht out there," said Max, pointing.

About a mile offshore they could see a large yacht at anchor. It was white and sleek with furled sails and wooden decks. They watched the little dinghy chugging towards the yacht until it drew alongside. A second person appeared on the deck to help tie up the dinghy, but they were too far away to get a clear view of what the other man looked like.

"Do you think the person we saw last night was signalling to the people on that yacht?" said Joe.

"Why would he do that?" said Lucy. "They could just bring the boat into the harbour and talk to him any time they want to. That doesn't make much sense."

"Unless they wanted to bring something ashore without being seen," said Max. "Something they didn't want the harbour authorities to know about."

"You mean they might be smugglers?" asked Charlie breathlessly. The word hung in the air, conjuring images in the children's heads of pirates and wooden chests filled with pearls and gold pieces.

Lucy frowned. "What would they be smuggling?"

"Barrels of rum," said Joe quickly. "And tobacco and spices and fine silks. I read all about it in a book on pirates."

"That was hundreds of years ago," said Max. "You can

buy all those things in the shops now. They must be smuggling something else. But what?"

"Well, we've got no way of finding out," said Lucy. She pointed out to sea. "They're out there, and we're stuck here. It's not like we've got a boat and can just sail over there and say, 'Excuse me, but could you tell us what you're smuggling, please?'"

The others laughed, but Joe looked serious. "I've got a boat," he said suddenly.

Lucy, Max and Charlie turned to look at him. "Do you mean some radio-controlled toy that your dad bought for you?" said Charlie. "Be serious for once, Joe."

"I am being serious," insisted Joe. "I *have* got a boat. Well, it's my dad's, really. He bought a motorboat at the same time as he bought the beach hut. He had some idea that we were all going to spend all our summers out on the sea. But he's never here, and my mum gets seasick. So most of the time it just sits idle."

"Where is it?" said Lucy.

"In a private boathouse, just up there," said Joe, pointing. "We could take it out to have a look at that big yacht and see if we can find any clues. It would be just like being real detectives or secret agents."

Charlie snorted. "You watch too many movies," she said. "We can't sail up to them in broad daylight. They'd see us coming for miles."

"We could go tonight, after dark," said Joe excitedly. "Then when we get close to the yacht, we can turn off the engine and row the last bit so they don't hear us."

"I don't know about that," said Lucy. "Taking out a motorboat at night sounds pretty dangerous."

"Dad made sure I had the safety training when he bought the boat," said Joe. "He thought it would be a good idea. And we've got all the safety equipment. We'll be perfectly safe, I promise." He looked at them all pleadingly. "Come on, it'll be fun."

They fell silent while they contemplated the prospect of a midnight motorboat ride to investigate the possible smugglers. It certainly sounded pretty exciting to Max. He could see that Charlie and Lucy were thinking the same thing.

"Alright," said Lucy eventually. "I guess it can't do any harm to go and have a *little* look. What's the worst that can happen?"

"Great!" said Joe, thumping his fist into his palm. "I'll go home and get the keys and meet you here this evening. Quick, everyone give me your phone numbers so I can let you know when I'm on my way."

They pulled out their phones and exchanged numbers. "Good," said Joe when they were done. "I'll head down here straight after dinner. I'll drop you all a message when I'm on my way."

"But make sure your mum says it's okay," said Lucy sternly. "I don't want to be accused of stealing someone's motorboat."

"Of course I will," said Joe, as though it was the most obvious thing in the world. "What do you take me for?" He began to back away from them, heading towards the car park. "I'll see you here tonight." He began to sprint away. Then he paused and looked back.

"And don't worry," he shouted to them. "It'll be fine. You can *trust* me."

8

THE SEA QUEEN

That evening they converged again on the harbourfront, under cover of darkness. Max rolled up on his electric skateboard and found Lucy, Charlie and Sherlock waiting for him.

"So where's Joe?" he said as he glided to a halt. "He messaged me to say he was on his way, but that was ages ago. He hasn't stood us up, has he?"

"I wouldn't put it past him," said Charlie. She shivered and pulled her fleecy jacket tightly around herself. Now that the sun was gone, the night air was bitter, and the moon cast a soft silver light behind thin clouds.

"Well, I hope he hasn't," said Lucy. "I told my dad I was going to the gym this evening. I'll be in all sorts of trouble if he finds out I'm not there."

"Me too," said Max. "I had to creep out while my folks were watching TV so they didn't see me leaving with all this stuff." He hefted the large backpack he was wearing. It looked like it was full of something very heavy.

"What have you got in there?" asked Lucy.

Max tapped the side of his nose conspiratorially. "Just a few bits and pieces from the stockroom," he said. "Things that every modern detective needs. You'll see."

Lucy frowned. She didn't like it when Max was being mysterious, but, before she could ask any more questions, Joe arrived. He looked like he had run all the way from his house. He was pink in the face, and his eyes were gleaming with excitement.

"Sorry I'm late," he gasped. "I had to wait for Mum to go out before I could leave. She thinks I'm staying in to do my homework."

"Did you get the keys?" asked Max expectantly.

Joe fished in his pocket and pulled out a bunch of keys that gleamed softly in the moonlight. "Come on," he said. "The boat shed's just up here."

He led them past working fishing boats that had been secured for the night and rows of gulls hunched down on the boat shed roofs. They travelled in a line, nobody speaking as they moved swiftly through the boatyards, keeping to the grass verges to deaden the sound of their footfalls and feeling more like secret agents with every step. Even Sherlock seemed to know that he was meant to be quiet as he snuffled along at Charlie's heels.

About halfway along the harbour front they passed by the harbourmaster's office, a stern black shed bristling with warning signs and a notice board listing the harbour regulations. The office windows were dark.

"That means that Creech is out on his rounds," said Joe. "We'll have to keep an eye out for him."

"I thought you said you had permission to take the boat out," said Lucy.

"I do," said Joe at once. "But you know what Creech is

like. If he caught us, he'd probably want to phone our parents to check. Do you want him doing that?"

Max and Lucy agreed that they did not, although Charlie didn't look like she much cared. Max wondered how it was that she seemed to come and go as she pleased. Didn't her mum and dad care what happened to her?

A little way beyond the harbourmaster's office, a small boathouse with green-painted doors lay close to the water. A concrete slipway led from the boathouse to allow a boat to be wheeled down to the water's edge. "It's in here," said Joe. There was a heavy padlock on the door, and Joe fumbled with the keys, trying several in the lock without success. The others formed a tight huddle behind him, peering over his shoulder and buzzing with excitement.

"Can't you get a move on?" hissed Max. "Someone will see us."

"I'm going as quick as I can," snapped Joe. "Perhaps if you all stop crowding me."

"What about that key?" asked Lucy. "It looks like it might fit."

"Quiet!" hissed Charlie from the back. "There's someone coming."

Everyone stopped talking and held their breath. The sound of steady footsteps could be heard crunching along the gravel path towards them.

Charlie stuck her head around the side of the shed to take a look. The wide cone of a torch beam was swinging from side to side as it came along the path. Then she saw a skinny shadow in a peaked cap, holding the torch.

"It's Creech!" she hissed. "And he's coming this way!"

They all slipped into the shadows and pressed tightly against the doors of the boathouse, hoping that Creech wouldn't catch sight of them. The footsteps came closer and closer until they were level with the boathouse, and then, horror of horrors, they stopped. Max caught Lucy's wide-eyed expression as the torch beam shone along the side of the boathouse and illuminated the concrete slipway barely a metre from where they were hiding.

"Who's there?" came Creech's nasally voice. "Come on. I know there's someone down there."

Max's mouth went dry, and his heart thumped like a rubber mallet in his chest. He felt sure that Creech must be able to hear it. Lucy clamped a hand across her own mouth to stop herself from making a noise, and Joe squeezed his eyes tight shut as though that might keep him hidden. Charlie crouched in front of Sherlock and raised a warning finger. The little dog seemed to understand and kept dead still.

Creech's footsteps started down the slipway towards their hiding place. But, just when they felt sure they would be discovered, a gull that had been nestling on a piling stirred itself and took to the air with a wheezy cry.

There was a startled shout from Creech as the bird took off, and he whirled around, tracking the bird with his torch. Then he grunted and muttered something under his breath. The torch snapped off, and a moment later, they heard his footsteps fading back down the gravel path.

The children let out a collective sigh of relief. "That was too close for comfort," gasped Joe.

"Hurry up and get this door open before he decides to come back," hissed Max.

Joe fumbled the keys again, and, this time, he got lucky. The padlock sprang open, and Joe hauled open the wooden doors. He fished a torch from his pocket and shone it inside the shed, and the children all gasped with delight.

Standing inside the shed was a small motorboat on a wheeled trailer. The boat was made of wood the colour of leather and honey, and there were two rows of seats upholstered in a shiny red. There was a white steering wheel and a tiny flagpole at the back, flying a Union Jack. Gold lettering on the front of the boat spelled out the name *The Sea Queen*.

"Awesome!" said Max.

"It's beautiful!" said Lucy in a hushed voice.

"She's a 1961 Chris-Craft Capri," said Joe proudly. "My dad said he paid an arm and a leg for it."

"I'm surprised your dad's got any arms and legs left," said Charlie.

Max ran his fingers along the smooth wood. It felt warm to the touch, like a living thing. "Are you sure you know how to drive this?"

"Of course," said Joe. "I told you, my dad made me do all the safety training. The weather forecast is fine, and there's fuel in the engine. There's life jackets under the seats, and I've got everything else we need right here." He pulled off his own rucksack and threw it into the back of the boat. "There's an air horn, some whistles, a torch, a first aid kit and a couple of flares."

Lucy grinned. "You weren't kidding," she said. "You really have done the safety training, haven't you?"

Joe flushed with pride. "You can't be too careful at sea," he said. "Now help me get her down to the water."

Together they picked up the front of the trailer and wheeled the boat gently down the slipway to the river. While Max held the mooring rope, the others pushed the trailer into the water until the boat floated free. They were wet up to their knees, but nobody cared. They were all too anxious to get started.

While Joe locked up the boathouse again, the others

climbed into the boat and settled on the comfy red seats. It took a while for Charlie to lift Sherlock inside. "Blimey, Sherlock. You really are heavy for such a small dog," said Charlie as she handed him up to Max.

At last, they were all on board and ready to leave. Joe sat in the driver's seat with Lucy next to him while Charlie and Max sat in the back with Sherlock between them. Joe made them all put on their lifejackets and made a great show of checking that they were fastened correctly. There was even a dog-sized life vest for Sherlock, which he sniffed at dubiously while Charlie put it on.

"If I start the engine, old Creech will hear it immediately," said Joe. "We'll have to paddle quietly out of the harbour."

He took two paddles from beneath the seat and handed one to Lucy, and together they dipped them into the water and began to paddle the boat. It took some time to get out to the middle of the river, but as soon as they did, the current began to carry them quite rapidly.

"It's a good job the tide's on the way out," said Joe. "Otherwise we'd never be able to paddle against the current."

The river took them quite swiftly now, and Joe and Lucy only needed to dip the paddles into the water occasionally to keep the *Sea Queen* in the middle of the flow. They fell silent as they passed the illuminated windows of the harbourmaster's office. "Creech must have gone inside for the evening," said Joe. "We'll be fine now."

In the back seat, Max relaxed and leaned back as he took a deep lungful of the sea air. There was something about being on a boat, he decided, that just made everything feel more adventurous. Then the boat lurched, and Max sat up with a start.

When they reached the mouth of the harbour, the waves

caught the little boat, slapping against the wooden hull and tossing it up and down like a rocking horse. Max clutched the sides of his seat nervously. Suddenly he was less sure about the adventure than he had been a minute ago.

Joe turned on the ignition and pressed the starter button. There was a slow whirring noise from the back of the boat that sounded like a creature in pain. Frowning, he tried again, with the same result.

"What's up?" asked Max. The motion of the waves was starting to make him feel seasick.

"The battery's a bit flat. Nothing to worry about," said Joe, sounding very worried. "It might take a moment to get going."

"Didn't you think to check it before we left?" hissed Charlie from the back.

"Well, I couldn't very well start the engine with Creech snooping around, could I?" snapped Joe.

"Can you stop it swaying about so much?" said Max. He was regretting the third helping of his mother's curry that he'd eaten before he left home. He was feeling decidedly queasy now.

Lucy glanced anxiously over her shoulder. The current had carried them some distance offshore. "Joe, what if you can't get it started?" she asked. "Will we be able to get back?"

Joe did not answer, but he was now starting to look even more worried. He stared at the ignition switch and pressed repeatedly on the starter button. Suddenly, the engine coughed and sprang to life. There was a brief roar and a rush of petrol fumes, and the engine settled to a steady purr.

Everybody breathed a sigh of relief, and Joe broke out into a huge smile. "I knew it!" he cried. "I knew there was nothing to worry about." The others looked at him with the expressions of people who knew that there had been quite a lot to worry about.

Now that the engine was running, Joe pushed on the throttle and steered the boat into the waves. The boat began to skip lightly between the peaks, and Max's queasiness began to recede. Sherlock put his paws up on the seat between Joe and Lucy and let his ears stream backwards in the breeze. Even Charlie was smiling.

"This is brilliant, Joe," said Lucy. "I can't understand why your mum doesn't like boats."

"She likes them well enough when she goes on holiday to places like Italy," said Joe. "But she doesn't really like anything about Southwold."

"Well, I think this is the best way to travel, ever," said Max. "Do you think we could get all the way to France in this thing?"

"Not without a lot more petrol," said Joe.

"I'd settle for just getting to that yacht and back without Joe's boat conking out on us again," said Charlie.

Joe steered steadily towards the yacht, and they could now see how big it was. "She's a beauty," said Joe as they drew nearer. "She's easily an eighty-footer. She could probably sail halfway around the world if she wanted to."

They could see that the yacht was securely anchored, and the rubber dinghy they had seen earlier was now tied up on a long rope behind it. There was no sign of anyone on the deck, but there were lights inside the cabin, and one of the portholes in the side of the boat was open. "Better cut the engine before they hear us," said Max.

Joe duly turned off the engine, and the little boat fell quiet. As soon as the noise died away, they heard the sound of loud music coming from inside the boat. "Well, they're definitely home," said Max. "Can you get us any closer?"

"Grab the paddle, Lucy," said Joe. "Let's go carefully though. If they spot us, we'll have to pretend that we're just out on a night-time fishing trip."

"Yeah, because we all look just like fishermen," said Charlie sarcastically.

Joe ignored her and picked up his own paddle. He and Lucy tried to propel them forwards without making too much sound, but as they drew closer, it was obvious that the music inside the yacht was too loud for anyone to hear what was going on outside.

Joe guided them expertly alongside the yacht, not touching, but close enough that they could look up at the open porthole. The sound of muffled voices was coming from within, but they couldn't make out what was being said over the noise of the music.

"Now what?" asked Charlie. "We're not going to find out

anything like this. We might as well turn around and go back before someone spots us."

Joe opened his mouth to reply, but, before he could speak, the music snapped off suddenly, and there was silence save for the slapping of the waves.

"Quiet," hissed Lucy. "If we make a noise now, we'll be rumbled!"

9

SMUGGLERS!

T he children stared at each other in horror as their boat bobbed next to the yacht. Max could see that what Lucy had said was right. Now that the music had stopped, the slightest noise would give them away. He was about to signal to Joe that they should start using the paddles to move away as quietly as possible when they heard voices talking inside the yacht again. This time they could hear what was being said very clearly.

"Oi!" said an angry voice. "I was listening to that." The voice was rough and filled with menace, and Max guessed it belonged to the scruffy man they had seen in the dinghy.

"You call that music, Sharkey?" said a second man. His voice sounded completely different. He spoke very clearly and with a refined accent. Joe thought he sounded like the people his mum and dad had over for dinner parties sometimes.

"That's just a horrible noise. Besides, I don't pay you good money to lie around on my boat while there's work to be done."

"I've done all me work," said the man called Sharkey. "I fetched the supplies from the harbour, and I washed the decks, like you asked. Aren't I entitled to a bit of peace for five minutes?"

"You're forgetting that we've still got merchandise to be delivered, Sharkey," snapped the first man. "Did you speak to that friend of yours? What was his name? Dean? What happened to him last night? He was supposed to meet us. You told me he was reliable."

"I saw him earlier while I was out getting supplies," said Sharkey. "He said it wasn't his fault." He sounded apologetic. "He said he was there on the sea wall at the right time, but he got attacked by a dog."

"A dog?"

"He said it was massive," replied Sharkey. "A Great Dane or an Alsatian or something. He said it nearly took his leg off. He was lucky to get away with his life."

Outside in the darkness, the four children looked at each other and then at Sherlock. They all knew he had sharp teeth, but it was difficult to see how anyone could mistake him for a Great Dane.

"Well, it's not good enough!" snapped the posh man. "I need to offload that merchandise before it goes off. The moon's too bright to try again right now, but as soon as we get a cloudy night, I want that merchandise off my boat. And no mess-ups this time!" His voice turned icy cold. "Otherwise you'll have bodies to dispose of, Sharkey."

Joe gasped and clamped a hand across his mouth to stop himself from making any noises. The others looked at each other, wide-eyed with terror.

Bodies! thought Max. The man was actually talking about disposing of bodies. His head swam.

With a panicked expression, Joe suddenly grabbed the paddle and signalled to Lucy to do the same. Trying to avoid making a splash, they paddled the *Sea Queen* backwards through the water until they were several metres away from the yacht.

"Wait, wait," said Max in a whisper. "Where are we going?"

"Away from here," hissed Joe. "Just as fast as we can. Didn't you hear what that guy said? They're smuggling something, and they're talking about disposing of bodies too. They're not just smugglers, Max, they're murderers!"

"We don't know that," said Max. "They could have been talking about anything."

"We know it well enough, Max," said Lucy. "These men sound really dangerous. We can't just pretend it didn't happen. We should tell the police."

"Tell them what?" asked Max. "That we were creeping around outside somebody's yacht in the middle of the night, and we think we overheard them talking about murder? The police would just laugh at us."

"Will you lot keep it down!" snapped Charlie. "If those guys hear us, we'll be in big trouble. We ought to be putting some distance between us and that yacht."

"Just hang on for a minute," said Max, raising his hands for calm. "I'm just saying we need more evidence if we're going to prove that they're smugglers or murderers."

"What are you suggesting, Max?" asked Lucy.

"We need to find out when they're going to try to bring that merchandise ashore again," said Max. "Then we can tell the police, and they can catch them red-handed."

"How are we going to find that out?" asked Charlie. "We can't very well watch their boat every night, can we?"

"Perhaps we can," said Max, with a smile. He began to rummage in his backpack. "I've got something in here that might help." He pulled out a device about the size of a tin of beans. There was a small circuit board connected to a battery and an old-style mobile phone. The whole collection of items was stuck together with thick wrappings of black insulating tape.

"What the hell is that?" asked Charlie. "It looks like a bomb!"

"Home-made tracking device," said Max proudly. "The mobile phone picks up the GPS signal, and the circuit board's been modified to run the tracking software. The battery should be good for about a week." He grinned as he hefted the device in his hand. "I can track the whole thing from the computer in my bedroom. If we hide it in that dinghy, I'll know as soon as they head towards the shore."

The others stared at the device in Max's hand. "I have no idea what any of that means," said Charlie, "but if that thing does what you say it will, then you're a genius."

The genius shrugged. "Well, I guess there has to be some upside to being short and fat."

"It's incredible," said Joe. "It really will be like being secret agents. How long will it take to plant it?"

"A few seconds," said Max. "Bring us a bit closer to the dinghy. And keep the noise down."

Joe and Lucy picked up the paddles again and rowed them closer to the rubber dinghy. The boat was tied to a long rope strung out at the back of the yacht, and it was easy to pull it alongside without alerting anyone inside as to what was happening.

Lucy kept an anxious eye on the yacht as Max carefully threw his leg over the side of the *Sea Queen* and stepped down into the dinghy. The rubber boat rocked violently, and Max had to bend his knees to avoid being thrown into the water. He crept to the back of the boat and reached under the dinghy's bench seat. He took out some old rags to make some space and then placed his device under the seat, remembering to switch it on first. After he had replaced the rags, he leaned back to admire his handiwork.

"Perfect," he said. "No one will suspect a thing."

"Okay, then," said Joe. "Get back in here, quick."

Max turned to leave but then paused. "Wait a minute," he said. "There's something here." A splash of colour in the front of the boat had caught his eye. There was something small and bright green lodged in a crevice beneath one of the front seats.

Watching from the boat, Sherlock's ears went back, and he let out a low growl. "Max!" said Lucy. "What are you doing now? We need to get out of here. Now!"

"One second," said Max. He bent down to retrieve the strange item and examined it in the half-light. Then he slipped it into his pocket. "Okay," he said. "I'm ready. Let's go."

He was halfway back inside the motorboat with one leg over the side when the dark sea turned suddenly to daylight, and an angry shout came from the direction of the yacht.

"You lot!" yelled the voice. "What the blazes do you think you're doing on my boat!" Two strong floodlights were turned on the *Sea Queen*. Blinded by the light, the children could see only shadows moving on the deck of the yacht, but they felt certain it was the two men they had heard earlier.

"Thieves!" shouted the angry voice. "Sharkey, stop them!"

Max's mouth went dry and his legs felt wobbly as he recognised the voice of the posh man. He looked around at his friends and saw they were all wearing the same terrified expressions. Even Sherlock looked afraid. The little dog's ears had folded back, and he crouched down low in the seat beside Charlie. Max wondered if there was still time to start the boat and get away, but one look at Joe told him the boy was frozen to the spot with fear.

"Sharkey! Bring them alongside," barked the man. "We'll show them what we do to thieves and vandals."

A moment later, a long boat hook connected with the front of the *Sea Queen*, making a large scratch on the wood panelling as the motorboat was dragged towards the yacht. Max looked around in horror, but there was no escape.

They had been caught by the smugglers!

10

DISGRACED!

Sharkey pulled the *Sea Queen* alongside the yacht and tied it up while the man with the posh voice barked orders at them. "All of you, get out of that boat and climb up here on the deck."

The posh man was stout and red faced with jowls that wobbled when he talked. He wore an expensive blue blazer, straining at the buttons, white trousers, and a nautical cap that looked brand new.

When they were all lined up before him, he glared at them while Sharkey stood behind him, holding the boat hook. "My name is Quentin De Havilland," he said with an angry shake of his jowls. "I'll have you know I'm a very important man in these parts, and I don't take kindly to young criminals trying to steal my property."

"W-we're not," stammered Joe. "I m-mean we weren't. We were just er " Joe realised he had no idea how he was going to finish his sentence.

"What Joe means to say," said Max quickly, "is that we were just out fishing, but then we broke down."

"A likely story," fumed De Havilland. "So how do you explain being in my dinghy? Come on, own up. You were trying to steal it, weren't you?" While he was speaking, his face became redder and redder until he looked like an over-inflated party balloon that was ready to pop.

Sharkey looked at the children through narrowed eyes. "I know this lot, boss," he said. "They were the ones who were watching me and Dean down at the harbour. I recognise that little rat of a dog." He pointed at Sherlock, who growled and bared his teeth in response to the insult. Charlie kept a tight grip on his collar.

"Keep that animal under control," snapped De Havilland. "He's a menace."

"Hey," said Sharkey suddenly. "You don't suppose they were listening, do you?" He nodded meaningfully to De Havilland. "When you and me were discussing *business*?"

De Havilland frowned and looked at the children thoughtfully. "How long were you all snooping around outside my yacht? Tell me the truth now."

"We weren't," said Joe quickly. "Snooping, I mean."

"We'd only just arrived when you came out and saw us," said Lucy.

"Why?" said Max. "Did we miss anything interesting?" He regretted his words almost as soon as he said them.

"Less of your cheek, lad," said De Havilland, turning several shades redder. Then he turned to Sharkey. "Get the dinghy ready. We'll hand them over to the harbour authorities and let the police deal with them."

The children gasped. "The police?" cried Lucy. "But you can't. I've never been in trouble with the police before."

"My mum'll kill me," said Max. "Dad got a parking ticket once, and she never let him hear the end of it."

Joe and Charlie said nothing. They just looked down at their feet.

A nasty smile crept across De Havilland's face. "How unfortunate for you all," he said gleefully. "Perhaps that will teach you a lesson; crime doesn't pay."

"We're not the ones who are the criminals," muttered Joe.

"What did you say?" De Havilland shot Joe a glare.

"What Joe meant to say," said Lucy, "is that none of us are criminals. If you just let us go, we promise we'll go straight home, and we won't bother you again."

But it was no use. The more they pleaded not to be taken to the police, the more De Havilland seemed to enjoy the prospect of doing exactly that. Sharkey pulled the rubber dinghy alongside, and De Havilland ordered them all to climb into it. Then, with Sharkey driving, they started back towards the harbour, towing the *Sea Queen* behind them.

"What are we going to do?" asked Joe miserably as they made the journey. "I'm going to be grounded until I'm middle aged."

"The one thing we can't do is tell the truth," said Max. He kept his voice down so that the two men could not hear him over the sound of the dinghy's outboard motor.

"What do you mean?" asked Lucy. "Surely you're not suggesting we lie to the police?"

"If we tell the police that these men are smugglers, they'll never believe us," said Max. "They'll just think we're making it up to avoid getting into trouble. And, what's worse, if these guys realise that we suspect them, then they'll just hide the evidence. The police will never catch them after that."

"He's right," said Charlie. "I don't know what they're smuggling, but they're definitely up to no good. Sherlock doesn't like them one bit, and he's never wrong about people. Until we've got some better evidence, we have to keep quiet about what we know, or they'll get away scot-free."

"Stop talking back there," growled Sharkey.

The four children stopped talking and sat in silence for the rest of the journey. As the boat ploughed through the waves towards the harbour, all of them were thinking the same thing. They were most definitely in serious trouble now.

When they arrived, De Havilland marched them triumphantly into the harbourmaster's office, with Sharkey following close behind. Creech was sitting behind his desk, eating egg sandwiches and drinking tea from a tartan-patterned thermos flask. He looked up when they entered, and his mouth dropped open in surprise, giving them all a view of a half-chewed egg sandwich. As soon as Creech saw De Havilland, he jumped up from behind his desk. He clearly knew who De Havilland was and treated him as someone of great importance.

"Mr De Havilland, sir," he said in a fawning voice. "What an unexpected pleasure. To what do we owe the honour of your presence?" He rubbed his hands together when he spoke, and a thin toady smile spread across his face.

When De Havilland explained why he was there, the harbourmaster's eyes widened with horror. He shook his head in disbelief and made disapproving noises. "Tried to steal your boat, you say?" he said in an outraged tone. "I knew they were trouble the moment I clapped eyes on 'em. Chased 'em out of my harbour this very afternoon, I did. Oh, you did the right thing bringing them to me, Mr De Havilland. I'll call the police immediately, and I'll have 'em safely behind bars in no time, don't you worry."

Creech's words made the children's hearts sink. Max wondered idly whether they served Christmas dinner in prison. While Creech telephoned for the police, Sharkey disappeared outside, seemingly anxious to be somewhere else when they arrived. Mr De Havilland took a seat in the corner, and Creech returned to his sandwiches, pausing occasionally to look up at the children and smirk in a very self-satisfied sort of way.

When the two policemen arrived, the younger one went outside to inspect the rubber dinghy and see if any damage had been done, while the older policeman began to question the children.

It took a long time to tell their stories. The policeman looked weary, like someone who has far more important things to do than deal with four children who had been caught creeping about on someone else's boat. He insisted on writing everything down very slowly in his notebook. While he wrote, he kept pausing to lick the end of his pencil, which Max thought was probably very unhygienic.

When he had finished writing, he read through his notes, frowning at the pages while the children stood in a line in front of the desk, looking shamefaced and miserable. "So," he said when he had finished, "tell me again what happened."

The children groaned. "We've already explained it..." said Lucy.

"At least three times now," added Joe.

The policeman looked down at his notebook and frowned. "Yes, you did," he said. "The only trouble is, your stories don't add up." He began to flip through his notebook. "You said you were out night fishing, but none of you has any fishing equipment. You said your engine cut out, but my officer could find nothing wrong with your boat. And you had no explanation at all for why you were found on board Mr De Havilland's dinghy."

"It's like I told you," said Max. "It looked like it was coming untied. I was just trying to make sure it was properly secure." Max winced when he told the lie. He was aware of how unbelievable their story sounded, but they had all agreed they could not tell the truth about what had happened. Not yet.

The policeman took off his glasses and rubbed his face wearily while Max wondered how many times the man would go on asking the same questions. He was just thinking how tired he felt and how much he wanted to be at home in his bed when the door opened and Joe's mother walked in.

Penelope Carter was an attractive woman whose face fell naturally into a disapproving frown. She swept into Mr Creech's office and descended on Joe like an angry bird. "Joseph Carter!" she shrieked as soon as she laid eyes on her son. "Just what have you been up to, you dreadful child? And who are all these *people*?"

She looked at Lucy, Max and Charlie as though she had found them lurking beneath her bins and was thinking of spraying them with disinfectant. She turned back to her son. "I was at a dinner party with the Hamilton-Browns when I got a call from the police. The *police*, Joseph. I could have *died* of embarrassment."

"Perhaps I could be of some assistance, madam," said Creech. As soon as he saw Penelope Carter, he had begun to preen himself, straightening his tie and smoothing back his hair. "The name's Creech," said Creech. "I am the Queen's Harbourmaster here, and it's my responsibility to–"

Penelope Carter pushed past Creech and approached the policeman sitting behind the desk. She turned on a glowing smile as though someone had thrown a switch. "Officer," she gushed. "Penelope Carter. Perhaps you could tell me what my son is supposed to have done? I'm sure there's a simple explanation, but if there's any damage, I'd be only too happy to pay..." She began to open her handbag.

The policeman held up his hand. "That won't be necessary, Mrs Carter," he said. "No damage as far as I can see. It seems your son took his friends out in your motorboat for a bit of a joyride."

"The motorboat!" Penelope Carter whirled around and fixed her son with a glare that felt to Joe like being under a magnifying glass in the sun. "How many times have we told you, Joe? You are *not* to take that boat without permission." The other children stared at Joe disbelievingly, remembering how he had assured them that he was allowed to take the boat whenever he wanted.

"So," said Penelope Carter, turning her smile back on the police officer. "What will happen to Joe now?"

The policeman shrugged. "Well, that's very much up to Mr De Havilland, madam."

Penelope Carter turned and caught sight of De Havilland for the first time. For a moment her eyes widened in surprise; then the smile flicked back on, twice as wide and twice as bright as before. "Quentin?" she said. "Quentin, is that really you?"

A large smile broke out on De Havilland's face. "Penelope!" he said, rising from his chair. "I thought I recognised your voice." He took her hand and kissed it lightly. "It's been so long," he said, "It must be five months since I last saw you?"

"Six," said Mrs Carter quickly. "At the golf club barbecue."

"Of course, of course," said De Havilland. He was all

smiles now, and his words oozed honey. "It's always such a delight to see you, my dear," he continued. Then he stole a quick glance at Joe and frowned. "It's just a shame it's under such unfortunate circumstances."

Penelope Carter glanced over her shoulder at her son and shook her head sadly. "I know, I know," she said. "He's such a worry to me. He runs completely wild. There's nothing I can do, and his father's no help." She pulled a lace handkerchief from her bag and dabbed the corner of her eyes. "I'm so sorry," she said with a sniff. "Sometimes I feel like I'm at my wits' end."

"There, there..." said De Havilland soothingly. He patted her arm. "I'm sure your boy will turn out alright in the end. He's just fallen in with a bad crowd, that's all." He turned his murderous gaze on Charlie, Lucy and Max. "Mark my words, a good dose of harsh punishment will sort that boy out. Just show him who's boss, and he'll soon toe the line."

At that moment the door opened again, and both Max's and Lucy's parents walked in, all four looking worried and frightened. Joy Green was a large Jamaican lady with a temper as fierce as a tropical storm. As soon as she saw Max, she took two strides across the office and grabbed him by the scruff of his jacket.

"Ow, Mum! You're hurting!"

"Maximillian Green, what is the matter with you?" raged his mother as she wagged her finger in his face. "Bringing shame like this on your family! What would your grandma say? Just wait until I get you home." Poor Max looked thoroughly miserable, and he stared down at the floor.

Ken Yeung stood at the door with folded arms and gave his daughter a frosty glare while his wife looked on sadly. "So this is what you get up to when we think you're at the gym?" he said in an icy tone. Lucy couldn't bear to look at him. "All those hours I've put into your training, Lucy, and *this* is how you repay me?"

Max's father, Tony, was introducing himself to Mr De Havilland. He was a mild-mannered man who liked to laugh, but tonight he looked like he carried the weight of the world on his shoulders. "We're so sorry for the trouble our son has caused you, sir," he said. "If there is anything we can do to make amends, please tell us what it is."

Max thought he would die of shame seeing his father apologise to Mr De Havilland. More than anything he wanted to blurt out that the man was a criminal, but he couldn't. They could hardly start changing their stories now.

De Havilland nodded gravely to Mr Green and then turned to the police officer. "So what will happen to these children now, officer?"

"That all depends on whether or not you want to press charges, Mr De Havilland," said the policeman.

De Havilland nodded again. "Yes. Yes, I see," he said. He glanced at Penelope Carter's tearful face and at the other anxious parents and then sniffed. "Well, I suppose there's not too much harm done," he said. "Thanks to the quick reactions of Sharkey and myself, we were able to intervene before any serious crime was committed. I'm prepared to let the matter drop as long as the parents agree to discipline their children properly."

"Oh, rest assured we will, Mr De Havilland," said Max's mum. "This boy's not going to be leaving his bedroom for the next month."

The other parents nodded their agreement.

"Very good," said De Havilland. "Well, in that case, I think we can call it case closed. Now if you'll all excuse me, I must be getting back to my boat. I'm sailing for France in the morning, and I shan't be back for at least a month. Good evening to you all." And with that he raised his cap briefly to Penelope Carter and left.

Ken Yeung looked at his daughter and held the door open. He gave a quick jerk of his head. "Go and get in the car, Lucy," he said. "We'll discuss your behaviour when we get home."

"Come along, Maximillian," said Max's father. "We also have some talking to do."

"Wait a moment, please," said Max suddenly. He turned to Charlie. "What about you, Charlie?" he said. "Your parents aren't here yet."

Charlie said nothing, but she looked furious. Her lips were clamped tightly together, and she stared straight ahead, not looking at Max.

"We spoke to Miss Wells's mother over an hour ago," said the policeman. He glanced down at his notes. "But she didn't seem too willing to come out."

Charlie bit her lip. "Mum doesn't like leaving the house after dark," she said. "I'll be okay to get home on my own."

The policeman sighed and pulled on his cap. "I don't think so," he said in a weary voice. "Come on, young lady. I'll run you home myself. I think I'd like a chat with your mother."

They started towards the door, but at the last moment Max darted forwards and pressed something into Charlie's hand. "Here," he said, "this is for you. I found it in the dinghy. I know you'll know what to do with it. It's up to you now." Then he turned and followed his parents out of the door, leaving Charlie and Sherlock alone with the policeman and Mr Creech.

Charlie stared after Max for a moment and then looked down at the thing Max had given her. Sitting in the palm of her hand was a feather. It was dark blue at the tip, yellow at the base, and multiple shades of green in the middle. It was like no feather she had ever seen before.

She stared at it for several seconds and then quietly put the feather in her pocket. And at that moment, she knew exactly what it was that Mr De Havilland and Sharkey were up to.

11

GROUP CHAT

*J*oe: Hello?

Joe: Hello?

Joe: Anyone there? Anyone at all?

Lucy: Hi.

Joe: At last. I've been messaging for two days now. No one answers.

Lucy: My folks took my phone away when they grounded me. I haven't been allowed to leave the house or talk to anyone all week.

Joe: What about your training?

Lucy: Dad borrowed a treadmill and put it in the garage. I have to look at a brick wall when I run now.

Joe: Grim.

Joe: So, apart from that, how did your folks take it?

Lucy: How do you think, Joe? They grounded me until after Christmas.

○ ○ ○

Joe: Bad luck. My mum took it pretty badly too. She kept going on about how much I'd embarrassed her in front of Mr De Havilland. Apparently, he's some sort of bigwig in the golf club, and now Mum thinks she's going to be a social outcast. She called up Dad just so he could shout at me over the phone, long distance. Then she took my phone away. Luckily I've got a spare she doesn't know about.

Lucy: My folks were furious too. At first, anyway. After that I think they were just in shock. They always thought I was such a good girl. I felt really ashamed.

Joe: You shouldn't feel ashamed. Every kid gets themselves into trouble at some point. It happens to me all the time.

Lucy: I didn't get myself into trouble, Joe. You did. You got all of us into trouble.

Joe: Me? How?

Lucy: *"Of course I have permission to take out my parents' motorboat. What do you take me for?"* – does that sound familiar?

Joe: Sorry. I just thought it would be fun. I didn't think it would end so badly.

Lucy: That's the trouble, Joe. You don't do much thinking, do you?

Joe: I said I'm sorry.

Joe: You still there?

Lucy: Yes. I'm still mad at you though.

Joe: Did you hear from the others?

Lucy: How would I? Dad only gave me my phone back today. Max is probably in the same position. His parents are even stricter than mine. I don't know about Charlie though.

Max: Hey. Did I miss much?

Lucy: Max! How are you? Is everything okay at home?

Max: Well, the hurricane is over, but now the ice age has begun.

Lucy: ?

Max: At first Mum wouldn't stop yelling. I lost track of the things she threatened to do to me. Now she's calmed down a bit, but she's stopped talking to me. She talks to my dad and to Saffy, but she pretends I'm not there. I think I preferred the yelling.

Joe: Don't worry, you just need to give her time to get over it.

Max: Thanks, but I need life advice from you like I need a hole drilled in my skull.

Lucy: How long are you grounded?

Max: Until New Year.

Lucy: That's harsh.

Max: Yeah, but at least they're letting me use my computer. That's how I logged on to the group chat. Something strange has happened.

Lucy: Nothing could be stranger than the last three days.

Max: You remember that tracking device I planted on De Havilland's boat?

Lucy: How could I forget?

Max: Well, I thought the police would have found it. But when I checked, I discovered it was still sending out a signal, and I began to track it. The day after he caught us, De Havilland's boat sailed away from the coast and disappeared out of range.

Joe: So what? He said he was going to France and he wouldn't be back for a month.

Max: Yes, but now he's back.

Lucy: What? How?

Max: I don't know. The signal just appeared again the night before last. He's anchored a couple of miles offshore. Not moving at all.

Joe: Why would he do that?

Lucy: I bet he's come back to finish what he started.

Max: Exactly what I thought. He still needs to offload his merchandise, and he's waiting for the right time to do it.

Joe: Is he still there?

Max: That's just it. The signal has just begun moving again. He's moved closer to the shore. I think he's going to do it tonight.

Lucy: Well, there's nothing we can do now.

Joe: We can't even tell anyone. They wouldn't believe us.

Charlie: *$&** Im here*

Lucy: Charlie, good to hear from you. You locked down too?

Charlie: no mymum wdnt dre try it. Bt she ws hrrble 2 S.lock tho – it ws awfl…$.

Joe: Are you okay, Charlie? Your messages aren't making much sense.

Charlie: I cnt hlpit $ itsa chep phone & its dffcult 2 typ txts on it.

Lucy: Well, I'm just glad you're alright. Is Sherlock okay?

Charlie: Ys hes fne thk gdness. Listn – I ned to tell u smthnng. Is Mx ther?

Max: I'm here. Where else would I be?

Charlie: I chckd out tht feathr u gv me. The ı u found on the boat.

Max: What about it?

Charlie: Its not frm hre, its v rarre. Then I figurd it out. I kno what dehavlland is up to. we hv to stp him.

Lucy: Stop him doing what? We can't understand you, Charlie.

Charlie:

Lucy: Charlie? Are you still there?

Charlie: Sry – Rlly bad wifi hr. I cnt explain properly rt now. But I thnk de havvlland mght be cming bk sn.

Max: He is coming back soon. In fact, I think he's coming back tonight. I've been tracking his boat.

Joe: Charlie? Are you still there?

Charlie: Im thnkng#

Charlie: I thnk Dehavvland is goig to unlod his merch tonite. We hav to try & stp him.

Lucy: Stop him how, Charlie? We're all grounded in our bedrooms.

Charlie: Well u nd 2 get out smhw. I'll mt you by the sea wall wher we met the ıst nite.

Max: Charlie, we can't get out. What part of grounded don't you understand?

Charlie: I dnt care – ths is mor impt. Lives r at stake. I tht u wr my frnds?

Lucy: We are your friends, Charlie. But what do you mean, lives are at stake? Whose lives?

Charlie: Jst come & Ill xplain whn u get hr.

Max: Like we said, Charlie, we're all grounded. We can't get out.

Charlie: Fine. if u wnt help me ill go by mself. CU around.

Lucy: Charlie, don't do anything stupid. Those men are dangerous. You can't go on your own.

Max: Charlie, are you still there?

Joe: I think she's turned off her phone.

Lucy: I'm worried about her. If those men really are coming back, she might get herself into serious trouble.

Max: Well, what can we do? I wasn't lying about being locked in my room.

Joe: You should do what I do when I want to get out without being seen. I climb out of my bedroom window.

Max: Climb out the window? Have you seen how short my legs are?

Joe: I'm serious. I can climb out onto the swimming pool roof and get down from there.

Lucy: Not all of us have swimming pools, Joe.

Joe: I know. But my dad has a ladder round the back of the house. I could bring it over to your place, and you could use that. It will be fine. Trust me.

Max: I seem to remember you saying something like that that shortly before WE ALL GOT ARRESTED!

Joe: Look, I know I messed up before. And I understand if you and Lucy don't trust me. But Charlie is our friend, and I'm worried too. I'm afraid she'll end up in serious trouble.

Max: I hate to admit it, but you've got a point.

Joe: What about you, Lucy?

Joe: Lucy?

Lucy: I'm thinking.

Max: Well, don't think about it too long. I've just looked at my computer. De Havilland is on the move again. It looks like he's on the way to the sea wall where we saw the wrecker.

Lucy: Oh no! Charlie's out there by herself. Alright, let's do it. Joe, how quickly can you get over here?

Joe: Give me ten minutes. We'll be around for you straight after, Max.

Max: Great, another of Joe's adventures. I can hardly wait.

Lucy: I'm on the first floor at the back of the house. And, Joe?

Joe: What is it?

Lucy: Please hurry. Charlie's all on her own – I'm really frightened for her.

12

ESCAPE

T he girl ran through the deserted winter streets at the north end of town, cursing the cold weather, cursing the fact that she hadn't thought to bring a warmer jacket, and cursing the fact that she was on her own again. It had been nice to have friends, if only for a short while. But it always ended up the same way. Whenever you were beginning to trust someone, they always let you down. Always.

She glanced down at the little dog running at her side. He looked up and 'ruffed' at her. Sherlock had no notion of where they were going, but he was just happy to be with the girl he loved more than anything in the world. "If only all my friends were as loyal as you, Sherlock," she said with a smile.

Arriving home in the back of a police car had not gone down at all well with her mother. Brenda Wells was not fond of dealing with the police, or anyone else for that matter. She was happiest at home, alone, with her crystals and her tarot cards, making watercolours of drippy fairies. Left to her own devices, Charlie doubted her mother would ever think to buy food or clean the house.

So, when Charlie had been brought home by the police and they had lectured Mrs Wells about not letting her daughter roam the streets late at night, Brenda had been mortified. As soon as the police had gone, she ranted and raved at Charlie about how she worked her fingers to the bone to give her daughter everything (not true, thought Charlie) and how Charlie had absolutely no respect for her (partly true, thought Charlie).

Brenda had long since given up trying to discipline her daughter, but there was something she could do that always had an effect. By way of a punishment, her mother had locked Sherlock in the shed and hidden the key, refusing to let him out until Charlie had learned better behaviour. Poor Charlie was forced to feed her beloved pet by pushing his food under the door and to sit outside while she listened to his pitiful whining.

She had tried to take her mind off Sherlock's dilemma by researching the feather that Max had slipped into her hand the other night. It had taken her some time to identify because it was so unusual, but as soon as she had found it in her book on South American birds, she knew it was the right one. It confirmed everything she had suspected about De Havilland and his creepy accomplices.

Her first instinct had been to tell her friends. After all, that was what friends were for, wasn't it? To give you help when you needed it? But instead she had just grown angry as she listened to their excuses. Why couldn't they understand how important this was? If a friend needed you, you were supposed to drop everything to help, weren't you?

At least there was one friend who would never let her down. A few swift kicks was all it had taken to break open the shed door. Then she and Sherlock were free, running through the streets and heading for the sea wall. She knew she had to hurry. If her suspicions were right, then, just like she had told the others, lives were at stake.

As she and Sherlock crossed the car park by the boating lake and approached the sea wall, they slowed to a walk. She could tell by the sound of the waves that the tide was out. She clambered up onto the concrete wall and looked out over the darkened sands to the granite rocks where Sherlock had fallen and so nearly been drowned. Was that really only a week ago?

Her heart sank. When she had learned from Max that De Havilland's boat was on the move, she had been sure she would see the ghostly fisherman standing on the granite blocks, waving his lantern, just as they had seen him on the first night. But there was nothing to see save for the waves crashing against the rocks. She had been wrong.

And then she saw it. Out at sea, a solitary light blinked once in the darkness. It was hard to tell how far away it might be. She climbed down off the wall and got out of sight in the deep shadows. The light blinked again, and again, and she realised that it was a small boat heading inland, right towards the spot where she was hiding.

She heard the faint sounds of an outboard motor and saw a dark shape pushing through the breakers as it headed towards the beach. There could be no mistake now. It was the same dinghy that Max had placed his tracking device in only a few nights ago, only now the boat appeared to be laden with boxes. De Havilland had returned to deliver his merchandise.

She watched carefully as the dinghy drew closer to the beach, and bit her lip. Should she run now to fetch the police so they could catch De Havilland red-handed? Or should she wait until her suspicions were confirmed and she saw them unloading the goods? And where was the ghostly fisherman they had seen signalling from the beach that first night? Something about this didn't feel right.

Sherlock barked once. "Quiet," she hissed.

Sherlock barked again, louder this time. "I said quiet!" She looked down at him and frowned. "You'll give us away."

"It's too late for that, girly!"

Charlie gasped at the sound of the harsh voice suddenly close behind her. A big hand grabbed her by the shoulder and whirled her around roughly, and she found herself face to face with the dark fisherman.

His features were hidden in the shadows of his black oilskins, but she could see quite clearly that he was not a ghost or a spectre. He was just a man. The man bared his bad teeth in a snarl. "I thought some of you kids might be back to do some more snooping," he growled. "So I lay in wait for you. Looks like I caught you and your nasty little rat of a dog."

"Let me go!" yelled Charlie. "You've got no right to do this." She tried to struggle, but the man was too strong for her.

Sherlock was barking madly at the fisherman now. The man glanced down and aimed a kick at the little dog, but Sherlock ducked out of the way and backed out of range of the man's boot. Keeping hold of Charlie with one hand, the man picked up a stone and hurled it in Sherlock's direction. It struck the dog on the rump, and he turned and fled into the darkness with a yelp.

"Sherlock!" screamed Charlie. She tried to kick out at the man, but he was too strong for her. He grabbed Charlie by the scruff of her jacket and lifted her so that her feet were very nearly off the ground. Then he marched her towards the beach, where the boat was just coming in to land.

"Get moving, you," he snarled. "Now you'll find out what Mr De Havilland does to kids who stick their noses in where they aren't wanted."

THE TINY STONE bounced off the glass with a barely audible *ping*. A moment later it was followed by another. Then another. Then a handful of stones clattered against the window like hail on a tin roof. "Lucy! Are you up there?"

The window was thrown open, and Lucy's head stuck out. She was wearing a black tracksuit with her hair tucked up into a black beanie. "Quit making so much noise down there," she hissed.

Joe stepped out of the shadows and grinned up at her, pushing his long blond hair out of his eyes. "I've been trying to get your attention for ages."

"My dad was in the next room," she answered. "I had to wait until he went downstairs. Did you bring the ladder?"

Joe reached into the shadows and proudly pulled out the pair of stepladders he had brought with him, placing them on the ground beneath Lucy's window. They were about five steps high and barely reached the ground-floor windows, let alone Lucy's bedroom.

"Is that it? How am I meant to get down with that?"

Joe shrugged. "Sorry," he said. "I thought it would reach further."

Lucy rolled her eyes. "Oh boy, you'd be useless in a prison break," she said. "My cat would be more help than you. Just get out of my way."

She swung a leg over the windowsill. "What are you doing?" asked Joe in alarm.

"Escaping from my bedroom without your help," she replied.

Lucy held on to the window frame with one hand and reached along the wall for the iron drainpipe that ran down from the bathroom next to her bedroom. When she had curled her fingers around it, she placed the sole of her trainer on the wall and swung herself out of the window, grasping the drainpipe with both hands as she did. Joe watched with admiration as she climbed swiftly down the pipe, moving hand over hand like a squirrel.

She jumped the last metre and landed beside Joe, who was staring at her wide-eyed with admiration. "Wow!" he said. "I don't know any girls who can climb as well as you."

"That's because you don't know any girls, Joe," said Lucy with a smirk. She brushed a loose strand of hair from her face and checked her watch. "Okay, let's get moving," she said. "If my dad discovers I'm gone, I'll be grounded until I'm a little old lady."

They picked up Joe's ladder and sprinted along the alley behind Lucy's house. At the main road, they headed down the hill towards the parade of shops where Max's parents had their computer repair shop.

In another alleyway behind the parade, they located Max's bedroom. "Third one from the end," said Lucy. "The one with the *Warlocks and Dragons* stickers in the window."

Joe frowned. "*Warlocks and Dragons*?"

Lucy rolled her eyes. "What can I say? The boy's a hopeless geek."

At that moment, the window to Max's bedroom went up, and he looked out, blinking in the semidarkness. "Joe, Lucy, is that you?" he hissed. "Can you get me down? Where's the ladder?"

"Don't get your hopes up," said Lucy. "Joe's ladder turned out to be a bit of a disappointment. Can you get onto the flat roof?"

Max's bedroom looked out onto the flat roof of the stockroom at the back of their shop. It was a short climb down from the window, but Max looked at the roof dubiously. "My dad's in there doing some repairs," he said. "If I walk across it, he might hear me."

Lucy and Joe looked at the illuminated window of the stockroom and wondered how loud Max's footsteps might be to someone inside. "There's no other way," said Lucy in a whisper. "Just go as quietly as you can. I'll climb onto the rubbish bins and help you down from there."

"Give me a minute." Max disappeared inside his bedroom and then reappeared a moment later holding his shoes in his hands. Moving gingerly, he began to climb out of his bedroom window. It was not done as gracefully as Lucy's exit. Max put both legs over the edge of the windowsill and then turned onto his stomach and lowered himself down. There was a moment's pause while he had to unhitch his tee shirt, which had become caught in the window catch, and then he was standing on the flat roof with his shoes in his hand.

He hoisted his rucksack onto his shoulder and began to tiptoe across the flat roof. A sudden creak from the boards beneath his feet made him stop and hold his breath in terror. When it was clear that Max's dad wasn't coming out to investigate, he continued to the far side of the roof, where Lucy was already standing on the bins, waiting for him.

"Take my bag first," he hissed, handing down the rucksack. "It's got some things I might need."

Lucy passed the surprisingly heavy bag down to Joe and then went back for Max. "Lower yourself down from the roof with your arms," she called up to him. "Then drop. I'll catch you."

"You'll catch me?" said Max. "Are you kidding?"

"Just do it," snapped Lucy. "Charlie needs us, remember?"

Max shook his head disbelievingly. "Alright, but I'm warning you, I bruise really easily."

Moving very carefully, the boy lay face down on the roof and began to edge backwards. First his legs came over the edge, then his stomach until finally he was hanging by his arms, his feet just above Lucy's head.

"Wait until I get into a better position," said Lucy. "Don't let go."

"Did you say 'let go'?" came Max's muffled voice. "Okay then."

A moment later the rounded figure of Max dropped from the roof and landed right on top of Lucy. The bins toppled beneath her feet, and the pair of them went sprawling in the shop's backyard. Empty tins and bottles spilled across the yard, and a large tom cat streaked out from the shadows, hissing loudly as it escaped across the yard.

"You call that catching?" groaned Max as he sat up amidst the rubbish.

"You call that jumping?" snapped Lucy. "I told you to wait."

"But I thought–" began Max.

They were interrupted by the sound of a key being turned in the back door. "It's my dad!" said Max in a near hysterical whisper. "He's heard us. Run for it!"

Three shadows sprinted out of the yard and around the corner just as the door swung open and Tony Green stepped out. He stood for a moment, scanning the debris strewn across his yard. Then he placed his hands on his hips. "Damned cats," he muttered, and he went back inside.

The three children ran until they reached the far end of the alleyway. "Stop, stop!" gasped Max. "Please stop."

"Don't say you're out of breath already," said Lucy. "We've hardly gone fifty metres."

"It's not that," panted Max. "It's my feet."

"What's wrong with your feet?" asked Joe.

"I left my shoes behind," groaned Max. "On the roof. These stones are sharp."

"Max!" said Joe. "How could you be so stupid?"

"It's not my fault," insisted Max. "You guys were hurrying me, and I was worried about getting caught. I got flustered, that's all. What am I going to do? I can't run all the way down to North Parade in my socks. My feet will be in a terrible state."

Joe stared at Max. "Seriously? We're on the track of a ruthless gang of criminals, and you're worried about your *feet*?"

"It's not my fault if I have very tender feet," said Max earnestly.

Lucy rolled her eyes. "Hang on," she said. "We can use

this." At the entrance to the alley was a pile of black rubbish bags and an overturned shopping trolley. Lucy dragged the trolley off the heap and turned it over. "Alright, get in."

Max blinked. "What?"

"In the trolley, tender-foot boy," she said. "We'll have to wheel you."

Max saw there was no time to argue. With some effort he heaved himself into the wire basket and sat down, with his legs sticking out in front of him. Lucy and Joe took the handle and began to push the trolley along the street. The trolley squeaked like a box full of angry mice, and one of the wheels wobbled terribly, but at least they were moving.

"Are you guys okay?" said Max, in a shaky voice.

"We'll manage," said Lucy as they leaned into the hill. "But as soon as this thing is over, I'm taking you running. You have *got* to get in better shape."

13

SHOWDOWN

The trolley trundled squeakily along the seafront, past the entrance to the old pier, heading towards the sea wall. Joe and Lucy were pushing while Max jiggled around inside. "This-is-really-uncomfortable," gasped Max. He was struggling to hold onto the trolley with one hand while he tried to read his mobile phone.

"Oh, yeah?" snapped Lucy. "You really ought to try being on our end of things. Please tell me that we're nearly there."

Max squinted at the phone screen as it jiggled in his hand. "It's difficult to tell," he said. "The signal from the tracking device is getting really faint. I think the battery must be nearly dead."

"There's something coming this way," said Joe suddenly.

They stopped pushing and looked where Joe was pointing. Something small and white was running full tilt along the promenade towards them.

"It's Sherlock!" cried Lucy. "Come here, boy."

Sherlock ran to the three children, barking madly. He refused to allow any of them to pet him, but he ran around them in tight circles, making a huge noise. Then he ran back in the direction he had come from before returning and barking some more.

Max had clambered out of the shopping trolley and was watching the dog curiously. "I think he's trying to tell us something," he said. "I think maybe he wants to take us to Charlie."

"Oh no!" said Lucy. "You don't think something's happened to her, do you?"

"I don't know," said Max, tapping his phone. "But it looks like De Havilland's boat has just pulled up by the sea wall at exactly the same place we saw Joe's ghost for the first time. Come on, we can follow Sherlock, but let's go quietly."

Joe took off his belt and looped it under Sherlock's collar to use as a lead. "Come on, boy," he said. "Show us where to find Charlie."

Sherlock did not need telling twice. He took off along the promenade, straining at the belt-leash and dragging Joe along behind him. Lucy followed them closely while Max, shoeless, hobbled along some distance behind.

At the end of the promenade, Sherlock led them through the empty car park to the stretch of barren concrete behind the sea wall. When Max arrived, puffing and panting, the three of them peered cautiously over the wall onto the beach below.

The tide was out quite a long way, and they could see a dark stretch of wet sand where a large rubber dinghy had been hauled up out of the water. "That's it!" said Max, checking his screen again. "It's definitely De Havilland's boat."

Two men were unloading crates and stacking them on the sand while a third stood in the boat, handing out the boxes and casting suspicious looks towards the distant light of Southwold in case anyone approached from that direction. Lucy could not see any of them clearly in the darkness, but she felt certain that the man in the boat was De Havilland and that the other two were his accomplices, Sharkey and the man they had called Dean.

"Look, there's Charlie," gasped Lucy. One of the two men had reached behind some rocks and pulled out a small struggling figure with long plaits whose hands appeared to have been tied.

"Oh no!" said Joe. "They've caught her."

They watched Charlie, still struggling with the man, as she aimed a kick at his leg. Then they heard her voice shouting angrily above the noise of the waves. "Get your grubby hands off me or I'll break both your kneecaps!"

"It's Charlie all right," said Joe. "What are we going to do?"

"I don't know," said Lucy desperately. "We're no match for those three men, but if we go for help, I'm afraid of what they might do to her."

But there was someone who knew what to do. As soon as he saw his mistress struggling with one of the men, Sherlock leapt forwards, pulling the makeshift lead out of Joe's hands and bounding down the steps of the sea wall. Before Joe could stop him, he had leapt onto the sand and was running towards the three men, barking and snarling so loudly that he sounded like a whole pack of dogs.

The man holding Charlie looked up and cried out in surprise, and Lucy saw that it was definitely Sharkey. He raised an arm protectively just as Sherlock leapt and closed his jaws around the arm of his jacket. Sharkey let out a startled cry as he tried to shake the dog loose. For a terrible moment Sherlock dangled from Sharkey's arm as the panicked man tried to free himself.

Finally, Sharkey tore off his jacket and threw it to the ground with a yell. But Sherlock was not done yet. As Dean came to help his companion, Sherlock turned on him too, sinking his teeth into Dean's thigh.

Dean started screaming, and Sherlock turned tail and ran, sprinting away into the darkness before either man could stop him. "It's that damned dog again!" yelled Dean, clutching at his leg. "The same one as before. It's like some sort of hound from hell."

"Where did it come from?" yelled Sharkey. He was looking around fearfully, as though expecting Sherlock to come flying out of the darkness at any second. "If that dog's here, then those kids won't be far away."

"Over there, you idiots," shouted De Havilland from the boat. "They're standing beside the sea wall." He pointed straight at Lucy, Max and Joe, who were now standing in clear view at the top of the steps. "Get them!" he cried.

Sharkey and Dean started running towards the three children. "Uh-oh," said Joe. "They've rumbled us. Let's get a move on." The three of them turned and began to run, not daring to look back at the two men lumbering after them.

If Joe and Lucy had been on their own, they might have escaped easily. But poor Max was still wearing only his socks, and they had gone only a few metres when he cried out in pain. "My foot!" he yelled. "I've trodden on something sharp." He sat down with a bump and clutched his injured foot.

Lucy and Joe turned just in time to see the two men catch up with Max and hoist him up onto his feet. As Dean held on tightly to the boy, Sharkey shook his fist and yelled after Joe and Lucy.

"That's two of your friends we've got now," he shouted. "If you want to see either of them again, you'd better get yourselves back here right now!"

Joe's eyes opened wide. "What are we going to do now, Lucy?" His voice was trembling.

"We don't have any choice," said Lucy calmly. "We have to go back."

They walked slowly back towards the two men. Lucy's

heart was hammering in her chest as though she had run a half marathon, but she did her best to keep a calm expression. It wouldn't do to let these men see they were afraid of them.

Joe held up his hands and tried to force a smile. "We don't want any trouble, honest," he said. "We were just out for an evening walk. If you let our friends go, we'll be on our way."

Sharkey turned and spat on the pavement to show what he thought of that. "Out for a walk? D'you think I'm stupid?" he growled. "You're the same kids we found snooping around our yacht the other night. You were warned to keep away from us, and you didn't listen, so now we're going to have to do things the hard way. Come on."

He grabbed Joe and Lucy by their jacket collars and propelled them along in front of him as they walked back to the beach. Poor Max hobbled along as best he could, but it was obvious that his foot was hurting him a lot. "Are you okay, Max?" asked Lucy. "Did you cut yourself badly?"

"No talking," growled Sharkey. He prodded Lucy in the back. "Save it for when you see Mr De Havilland. He's going to have plenty of questions for you."

They descended the steps to the beach, where De Havilland was waiting by the dinghy. Charlie was sitting on the sand by some rocks, with her hands still tied in front of her. When she spotted Lucy, Max and Joe, her eyes grew wider and her jaw dropped. "You!" she said in amazement. "You decided to come after all."

"Hi, Charlie," said Joe as they approached. "We thought you might need some help."

"As you can see," added Max, "it's going really well so far."

Sharkey cuffed Max around the side of the head. "Shut up, you!" he snapped.

De Havilland scowled at the children. "I might have known the rest of you brats would be around here somewhere," he said. "So you couldn't resist coming back to stick your noses into my business again, could you? What are you, some sort of after-school detective club?" He paused to laugh at his own joke.

"We didn't mean to pry, honestly," said Lucy. "We were just curious, that's all. If you let us go, we won't tell anyone what we saw. Honestly we won't."

De Havilland glared at Lucy for a moment. Then he threw back his head and laughed. He laughed so long and so hard that Sharkey and Dean joined in until all three of them were laughing like madmen. "Do you think I was born yesterday, young lady?" he spluttered. "If I let you go, you'll run straight home to Mummy and Daddy to tell them what you've seen. Well, I'm conducting a business deal here, and I'm not about to let a bunch of spoiled kids like you interfere with it."

"We know all about your 'business deal'," said Charlie. "And I know exactly what you've got in those boxes."

Max, Lucy and Joe gave each other puzzled glances while the three men began to look distinctly uneasy. "You're lying," said De Havilland. "You've got no idea what's going on here."

"You're smuggling animals," said Charlie defiantly. "Species of rare and endangered birds, to be precise."

The three men looked horror-struck. "How come these kids know what we're doing, boss!" asked Sharkey "Someone must have talked."

"Shut up, you fool!" De Havilland's face had grown as dark as an approaching winter storm. "She's bluffing," he said. "It's nothing more than a guess. They've got no evidence."

"Max found a feather on board your dinghy," said Charlie. "It took me ages to identify it properly because it's not from a British bird. It's from a really rare South American parrot called a blue-throated macaw. They're nearly extinct in the wild, but people like you smuggle them into the country to sell to collectors for high prices. I read about what you do." She nodded towards the boxes stacked up on the beach. "If I'm right, then I reckon those boxes are probably full of wild birds, all crammed tightly together. It's a cruel and horrible thing to do, and lots of them die on the journey."

When Charlie had finished speaking, everyone fell silent, and they were suddenly aware of the sounds of rustling and muffled squawking. Joe, Max and Lucy stared at the crates, wondering how many creatures were crammed in there.

De Havilland's look of anger had gradually given way to one of surprise and then, finally, amusement. He stroked his chin thoughtfully. "You're a lot smarter than I gave you credit for," he said. "But you got one thing wrong. I don't just deal in rare birds. I import anything my customers want. Snakes, turtles, monkeys, I even brought in a baby tiger once. No one suspects a respectable businessman like me with his own private yacht. It's the perfect cover and *very* profitable."

"Well, it looks like your game's up, De Havilland," said Joe bravely. "Now we know what you're up to, it's only a matter of time before the police catch you."

De Havilland chuckled. It was the sort of laugh people make when they know something that you don't know. It made a chill run down Joe's spine.

"Oh dear," he said. "Perhaps you're not so bright after all." He pointed to the boxes. "I've got over a hundred rare birds and reptiles in those crates, and I have buyers waiting for all of them. Do you really think I'm going to let you go talking to the police?" He nodded to Dean and Sharkey. "Tie them all up," he growled. "After we've unloaded the goods, we'll take them back to the yacht and deal with them later."

Dean and Sharkey looked at each other nervously. "Er, I'm not sure about that, boss," said Sharkey. "That's kidnapping, isn't it?"

De Havilland's face twisted into a furious scowl, and he bared his teeth in a snarl that made Dean and Sharkey recoil. "You idiots," he growled. "We'll all go to prison for ten years if those kids tell the police what they know. Is that what you want?"

Dean and Sharkey both shook their heads.

"Good. As soon as we've finished unloading, we're sailing back across the channel. We'll take the kids to Belgium and dump them there. By the time they get home and tell their stories to the police, we'll be long gone. Now, do as I say and tie them up."

Sharkey looked unhappy, but he didn't argue. He collected a length of rope from the boat and began to cut it into shorter lengths. Dean wrapped a piece of the rough nylon cord around Max's wrists and pulled it tight.

"Steady on," said Max. "I've got very sensitive skin, you know."

Sharkey tied Lucy's wrists in a similar fashion. She grimaced as he pulled the knot tight but refused to cry out. Over Sharkey's shoulder, she noticed Joe. While no one was watching, he was reaching inside his backpack. He saw Lucy looking at him, and he winked. Lucy frowned. What on earth was he doing?

Dean shoved Max down onto the sand next to Charlie. Max turned to the girl and gave her a wink. "Well done for working out what they were smuggling," he said. "That was a piece of genius."

"Thanks," said Charlie. "But it was teamwork. I'd never have figured it out if you hadn't found that feather." She gave him a smile. "I'm sorry I got so angry with you all earlier. Thanks for coming to rescue me."

Max sighed. "For all the good it did. They're going to get away with it, and we're going to end up getting dumped in Belgium. I don't even speak Belg-ish."

"It's Belgian," said Lucy as Sharkey plonked her down on the sand next to them. "And don't worry. This isn't over yet."

Sharkey turned to Joe with a piece of rope in his hand. "You next," he growled.

Joe chose that moment to make his move. As Sharkey came towards him, the boy took a step backwards. "Stay away," he cried in a nervous voice, "or I'll use this." He pulled something from his bag, a thick red tube about the length of his forearm, which he held up with both hands.

"Dammit!" yelled De Havilland. "The boy's got a distress flare."

"And I know how to use it too," said Joe in a shaky voice.

As Joe's eyes flicked nervously between the men, Sharkey took a step forward. "Now, don't do anything stupid, son," he said. He narrowed his eyes and made a sudden lunge at Joe.

Several things happened in quick succession. There was a loud *pop* as Joe jerked the string hanging from the bottom of the red tube. There was a *whoosh* like the sound of a rocket on fireworks night, and a thin trail of smoke spiralled up into the sky. There was a distant *bang*, and a red star burst like a dying sun over their heads, bathing the whole beach in blood-red light.

Sharkey staggered backwards in surprise, tripping over a pile of boxes that had been placed on the sand. "Damn you, boy," snarled De Havilland. "I'm going to make you regret that."

THE DIAMOND-BACKED
BOONDOGGLER

D e Havilland took three strides across the sand towards Joe, with fury in his eyes. Joe turned and tried to run but almost immediately tripped over one of the boxes lying in the sand. Joe tried to scramble away, and, for a moment, it looked as though De Havilland might hit the boy, but then Lucy cried out.

"Leave him alone," she yelled. "He's just a kid. Pick on someone your own size."

De Havilland turned and glared at Lucy, wild-eyed. Then he seemed to collect himself. He stepped back from Joe and straightened his jacket.

"You two," he barked at Dean and Sharkey, "get that last one tied up before he creates any more havoc. Then watch these kids while I go back to the yacht to collect the rest of the boxes."

"But, boss, what about that flare?" said Dean, pointing at the red star that was now descending slowly towards the beach. "The police will see it."

"Calm down, you idiot," said De Havilland. "It's only been a few weeks since fireworks night. If anyone does see it,

they'll just think that it's some kids messing around. Nobody
is going to come and investigate. Now wait here while I get
the rest of the merchandise, and don't let these kids give you
any more trouble." He threw the children a last venomous
glare before turning around and dragging the dinghy back
into the waves. A moment later he had started the outboard
motor and was chugging away towards his yacht in the
distance.

Sharkey finished tying Joe's hands, then dragged the boy
across the sand to sit next to his friends. "Joe!" said Lucy as
Sharkey shoved him down. "Are you okay?"

Joe looked dazed. His long blond hair was in disarray,
and there was a trickle of blood coming from his lip. But
he smiled faintly at Lucy and gave her a thumbs up with
one of his tied hands. "I hit my mouth on a stone when I
fell over," he said. "It hurts like anything, but it will be
worth it if the police saw the flare. Do you think they'll
come?"

By this time the bright red flare had dropped into the sea
and had been extinguished, returning the beach to darkness. There was no sign of anyone coming to investigate, let
alone the police. They all had a sinking feeling that De
Havilland had been right. If anyone had seen it, they had
probably just thought it was kids messing around. No one
was coming to help them.

Dean was still watching De Havilland's dinghy heading
back to the yacht. His face was pale, and he wore a worried
expression. "Now what are we going to do, Sharkey?" he
asked. "The boss is proper mad this time."

"We do what he told us to do," said Sharkey. "I'll watch
the kids while you go and get the van. And hurry it up, I
want to get these damn crates off our hands." He kicked at
the pile of boxes with the toe of his boot, and immediately

the sounds of rustling and squawking increased. It was clear that they were all crammed full of living creatures.

"Don't do that," cried Charlie. "They're just defenceless animals. Stop being so cruel to them."

Sharkey laughed. "It's nothing compared to what Mr De Havilland's going to do to you lot when he gets back," he said. "You won't all be so lively after a couple of days in the bottom of his boat."

A strange smile crept across Lucy's face. "You don't seriously think he's coming back, do you?" she said. "He knows the police are probably on their way here now. He's gone back to the yacht to make his escape, and he's left you two to take the blame."

Dean's eyes grew wider and more scared looking. "You don't think that's true, do you, Sharkey?" he said. "The boss hasn't gone off and left us, has he?"

Sharkey scowled. "Don't be an idiot," he said. "She's just winding you up, that's all. Take no notice."

Lucy fixed her gaze on Dean. "Think about it, Dean," she said. "He's left you here with all the evidence. There's nothing to connect him to the crime now. He can just deny everything."

"She's right, Sharkey," said Dean desperately. "He's left us with all these damned animals. If they catch us now, we won't be able to prove a thing."

Max, Joe and Charlie exchanged glances. They could see how much Lucy was unsettling Dean. The only trouble was that she also seemed to be making Sharkey very angry too.

"Shut up!" he snapped at Lucy. "Any more out of you and you'll get some of what your friend got."

Sharkey loomed over Lucy threateningly, but Charlie picked up where she had left off. "You know she's telling the truth, don't you, Dean," she said. "Better run now while you've got the chance. It'll be ten years in jail for you both if you don't."

"I warned you both," snarled Sharkey. "Now you've asked for this." He strode across the sand and grabbed the collar of Charlie's jacket and raised his other hand to strike her.

The girl gasped and put up her tied hands to fend him off. But at that moment, something flew out of the darkness behind her. It was something small, with sharp teeth and a huge heart. It was Sherlock.

After Sherlock had run away, he had not gone far. As soon as he was out of sight, he had circled around the group on the beach and lay in wait, watching for his chance to save his beloved mistress and her friends.

While the bad men were talking, he had crept back towards them. He'd approached under the cover of the rocks until he was no more than a few feet behind where the children were sitting. But when he saw Sharkey grabbing hold of Charlie, he could stay quiet no longer.

The little dog leapt from the shadows and seized Sharkey's outstretched hand in his jaws, closing his teeth on the thin skin between his thumb and fingers. Sharkey shrieked in pain, stumbling backwards into Dean before both men fell over the stack of boxes on the sand.

There was a crunch of breaking wood and a cacophony of screeching and shrieking from the animals inside. Several tightly bound packages rolled onto the sand, and Max gasped. What he was looking at were parrots, tightly bandaged so that they could not move their wings. When he looked closer, he was shocked to see that some of them had their beaks taped together to prevent them making a noise. There were at least a hundred of the birds crammed into the narrow box.

Dean sat in the centre of a broken wooden box and was screaming at the top of his voice. "The snakes!" he shrieked. "The snakes are loose." All around him was something that looked like a nest of tentacles, writhing and twisting and crawling all over him as he tried frantically to get away.

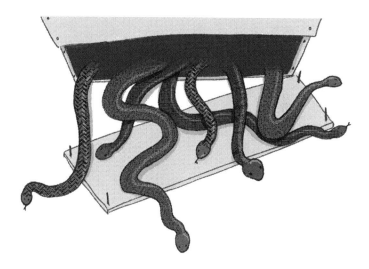

"Help me, Sharkey!" he wailed. "They've got me!"

Sharkey swore under his breath. Clutching his bleeding fingers, he glared around, trying to catch sight of Sherlock, but the little dog had disappeared back into the darkness. "When I catch that rat," he growled, "I'll wring its little neck."

"Sherlock's too brave and too smart for you to ever catch him," said Charlie. "As long as you keep holding us here, he's never going to leave you alone."

Sharkey looked like he might argue, but Dean's pleas were becoming frantic. "Sharkey, please help me!" he cried. "Get 'em off me! I'm terrified of snakes."

Sharkey swore again and then went to help his compan-

ion. With his good hand he pulled Dean from the wreckage
of the crate. Snakes of all sizes wriggled and squirmed to get
away from the broken box.

As Dean was being pulled to his feet, he let out a
hideous shriek of pain. "It bit me!" he wailed. "That one
bit me."

He pointed a shaking finger at a particularly fat serpent
that was slithering away across the wet sand. "That one bit
me!" he cried again. "What's going to happen to me now?"

Max watched the large snake crawling away, and an idea
began to form in his brain. "That's bad news, that is, Dean,"
he said, adopting a fearful expression. "That's a diamond-
backed boondoggler."

Dean looked as though he might faint on the spot. "A d-
diamond-backed b-b-boondoggler?" he said weakly. "Are
they p-poisonous?"

"Absolutely lethal," said Max with a deadly serious
expression on his face. "A single bite from a boondoggler
can kill a grown man in less than half an hour."

"Half an hour!" shrieked Dean. He turned in desperation
to his accomplice and grabbed hold of his lapels. "Help me,
Sharkey," he pleaded. "I've been bit by a boondoggler. Get
me to a doctor. I'm too young to die!"

Sharkey angrily shook himself free of Dean's grip.
"You're not going to die, you idiot," he snapped. "De Havil-
land said there were no poisonous snakes in this cargo.
You've got nothing to worry about."

"That's easy for him to say, Dean," said Max. "He's not
the one who's been bitten by a boondoggler. You'd better get
medical attention right away before your blood starts
turning to tar."

"To t-tar?" repeated Dean.

"Tell me," said Max, beginning to enjoy himself. "Is your heart racing?"

Dean thought for a moment. "Y-yes," he said. "It's thumping like a steam engine."

"And are you feeling sweaty?"

Dean felt his brow. "Y-yes," he wailed. "I'm sweating buckets here."

Max sucked his teeth. "That's bad, Dean," he said. "That's really bad."

"Shut up, you," snapped Sharkey. "Dean, calm down. He's just trying to frighten you. Trust me, that snake wasn't poisonous."

"You can't know that for sure," wailed Dean. He began to back away from Sharkey. "My blood might be turning to tar at this very minute. I've got to get to the hospital right away." He began to stagger backwards along the beach.

"Dean, calm down!" yelled Sharkey. "Nothing bad is going to happen to you. And we've still got a job to do."

Dean's breath was coming in hot gasps. "I've-got-to-get to a hospital," he said weakly. Clutching his bitten hand, he turned and ran away into the night.

"Dean, come back here!" yelled Sharkey. "We need your van to load the boxes." He swore again and began to chase after Dean.

The children watched the two men running away down the beach. "Right!" said Max, scrambling to his feet. "Everyone, start running."

15

CAPTAIN TOM TO THE RESCUE

T he others did not need telling twice. Moving as quickly as they could manage with their hands tied, they scrambled to their feet and began to run in the opposite direction to the two men, heading towards the lights of the town.

"A diamond-backed boondoggler?" said Charlie as she jogged along the sand beside Max. "There's no such thing. It was a baby python. They're completely harmless."

"I know that, and you know that," said Max as they ran. "But Dean doesn't know that. Do you think he's still running?"

At that moment a small energetic shape bounded out of the darkness towards them. Charlie immediately fell to her knees in the sand. "Sherlock!" she cried. "My brave, brave boy. You saved all of us back there."

"He's a real hero," said Lucy, kneeling down beside Charlie. "I don't think Sharkey or Dean knew what hit them."

Max and Joe quickly helped each other to unpick the knotted ropes around their wrists. The men had been in a hurry, and fortunately the ropes were not difficult to undo.

When they were free, they untied Lucy and Charlie, and then everyone joined in making a huge fuss of Sherlock.

The little dog had no idea what they were saying, but he knew that they were all very pleased with him, and that made him happy. As much as he loved his mistress, he had also missed her new friends over the last few days. He jumped around excitedly between the children, licking faces and rolling over in the sand to let his belly be tickled.

"We'd better get moving again," said Lucy, glancing over her shoulder. "They could be back at any minute. Are you okay, Joe?"

Joe dabbed at the small cut on his lip and he grinned. "It stings a bit," he said. "But I'll be fine."

"I'm not sure I will be, though," said Max. He had peeled off his sock and was examining his injured foot, which was cut quite badly. "I think I might have a piece of glass in it," he said, in dismay.

"We'll help you," said Lucy. "You can lean on me and Joe."

Lucy and Joe helped Max to get up, and placed his arms around their shoulders. Now that the initial excitement had worn off, poor Max's foot was really quite painful, and he had to hobble along slowly, supported by the others.

"Oh no!" said Charlie after they had gone a few yards. "They're coming back."

A hundred metres away, Sharkey was running up the beach towards them, closely followed by Dean. Dean had clearly got over his fear of being bitten by a boondoggler, and both men looked extremely angry.

"What are we going to do?" said Joe. "Max can't run with his bad foot."

"Go on without me," said Max quickly. "There's no sense in all of us getting caught."

"No," said Lucy quickly. "We're friends, aren't we? That means we all stand together, and we don't leave anyone behind. Do we all agree?"

Charlie and Joe nodded quickly, and Sherlock barked. "That settles it," said Lucy. "We'll make these two wish they'd never tangled with us."

They turned in a line to face the two men. Lucy, Joe and Max stood with clenched fists and grim expressions while Charlie held on to Sherlock's collar as they waited for the men to catch up with them.

When they were just a few paces away, the two men slowed to a walk. Sharkey scowled and bared his teeth. "You've done it now," he snarled. "Half of Mr De Havilland's snakes have escaped, and it's all your fault. He's going to be *very* unhappy when he sees you."

"Don't get any closer," yelled Charlie. "Not unless you want me to set my dog on you again."

Sharkey sneered. "That little rat?" he said. "He might have sharp teeth, but he's no match for this." He reached behind his back and pulled something long and heavy from the waistband of his trousers. Max recognised it as an iron crowbar, of the sort used for opening crates. "Let's see how brave he is after I hit him over the head with this a few times."

The children gasped at the sight of the vicious iron bar, and Charlie pulled Sherlock closer protectively.

"We're not afraid of you," said Joe. But they all knew it was a lie.

The two men were both grinning now as they approached. "You've caused us a whole heap of trouble," said Dean. "And now we're going to make you pay for it."

Max felt as though someone had filled his belly with ice water, his legs were shaking, and his mouth had turned completely dry. It had been his idea to try to catch these smugglers, he told himself. And now his friends were going to get hurt because of it. He could have kicked himself for being so stupid. This was all his fault.

He was still thinking this thought when the beach was suddenly filled with a blinding white light. For a moment, Max thought it was another flare. Then wide torch beams began sweeping across the sand from somewhere behind them. There was shouting and the sounds of several people running towards them. Somewhere overhead, they could hear the noise of a helicopter.

Max looked at his friends, but it was immediately obvious that they were as surprised as he was. A few yards away, Sharkey and Dean were wearing startled expressions as they shielded their eyes against the torch beams. Four men in blue uniforms ran straight past the children towards the two men.

"It's the cops, Sharkey!" cried Dean. "Run for it!"

The two men turned to flee, but almost immediately both were tackled to the ground by the police officers. Then the whole beach seemed to be filled with policemen. Two of them held on to Sharkey and Dean while another attached the handcuffs; others barked into radios or took notes in black notebooks. And nobody seemed to be paying attention to the children at all.

"What *is* going on?" asked Joe. He looked around at the others with a confused expression, but no one else had any answers.

"Ah, so there you all are," said a deep voice behind them.

They turned around to find themselves looking at a familiar figure walking towards them, swinging a walking stick. The man had white whiskers and was wearing a naval cap and a pea jacket. "Captain Tom!" chorused all the children together.

"That's me," said the captain, touching the peak of his cap. He glanced over at the two men lying face down on the sand. "I must say this looks like a nasty business," he said. "I'm very glad to find you all in one piece."

"Captain Tom, what are you doing here?" said Lucy. "And where did all these policemen come from?"

Captain Tom paused to lean on his cane and took out his pipe from his pocket. "I was up in the lighthouse, doing my rounds as caretaker," he said, pushing a plug of tobacco into the pipe. "When I spotted a group of children through my binoculars, heading towards the sea wall." His eyebrows knitted together in a thick hedge. "I wondered if it might be you lot after our conversation the other day. Then, a little while later, when I saw a flare go up from the beach, I began to get worried."

"We didn't think anyone had seen it," said Joe.

"I doubt that anyone did, apart from me," said Captain Tom. "Fortunately, I thought to call the police." He looked around. "As you can see, they came in force."

Suddenly, everyone wanted to ask questions at once.

"Why are there so many of them?" said Lucy.

"Do they know about the smugglers?" said Joe.

"Has anyone told them there are animals over there that need help?" said Charlie.

"Did they catch Mr De Havilland?" said Max.

Captain Tom held up his hands for silence. "Hold on, hold on," he said. "All in good time. I'm sure the police will want to talk to all of you, and there'll be plenty of time for questions. In the meantime–" he paused and glanced at Joe's split lip and Max's injured foot "–it looks like you lot have been in the wars. Let's start by getting you all somewhere warm and dry."

It turned out that Captain Tom's cottage was right on the seafront, close to the pier and near to where they were standing. Captain Tom spoke to one of the police officers, who appeared to be in charge, and then escorted the three children across the road to his house.

Captain Tom's wife was a round and jolly woman named Vera, who was completely unfazed by her husband arriving home with four children and a dog, and she fussed around them as she welcomed them inside.

"Come in, come in, my dears," she said, helping Lucy out of her jacket. "You're all soaked through and freezing cold too, I shouldn't wonder. And what on earth is going on with all them police out there? Smugglers, you say? Lordy, whatever next."

Half an hour later found them all sitting in Vera and Tom's front room, warming themselves by the fire while they sipped sugary tea and ate Vera's home-made scones and Captain Tom's special damson jam. Joe sported a huge lump on his lip, which he wore like a badge of honour as he explained for the third time to Captain Tom how he had got the injury escaping from the clutches of Mr De Havilland. Max sat with his injured foot in a bowl of warm water, to which Vera had added a cloudy splash of disinfectant, and Sherlock was crunching tea biscuits on the hearth while Charlie sat beside him and stroked him fondly.

They were interrupted by a knock at the door, and two men entered. The first was a large policeman in uniform, holding his cap in his hands. The children recognised him as the same policeman who had given them such a telling off in the harbourmaster's office.

"Not you lot again!" he said when he saw them. "I might have known you'd be at the bottom of all this. Didn't you learn your lesson last time?"

The children looked guiltily at one another and then at the policeman. Surely they weren't going to get into trouble again? Not after all they had been through this evening?

Lucy stood up. "We're sorry if we caused you any trouble," she said. "But we were sure those men were up to no good. We were just trying to find some evidence to prove it."

The policeman had turned quite red in the face and appeared to be very angry, but the second man laid a hand on his arm to silence him. "That will do, Sergeant," he said in a soft voice. The second man was tall and slim and wore a raincoat. He had a kind face but with steel-grey eyes that seemed to miss nothing. "My name is Inspector Callahan," he said. "And I'm very interested to meet the children who caught the notorious Jungle Crew."

"The Jungle Crew?" said Max. "What's that?"

The inspector accepted a cup of tea from Vera and nodded his thanks. There was a moment's pause while he sipped and made appreciative noises. "That was the name we gave to De Havilland and his gang," he said. "Some time ago, the police in London gave us a tip-off that they'd found a lot of rare creatures being sold illegally as pets. We suspected that there was a smuggling gang operating somewhere along this coast, but they always seemed to be one step ahead of us. Now we've caught them, thanks to you."

"But what about Mr De Havilland!" said Max quickly "He went back to his yacht before you arrived. You have to hurry, or he'll get away."

The inspector put down his cup and smiled as he

accepted a scone with jam from Vera. "Oh, don't worry about him," he said. "The coastguard caught him trying to escape across the channel. They found all sorts of wild creatures on board his boat. It turns out he's wanted in five different countries for smuggling endangered creatures."

"What's going to happen to all those poor animals?" asked Charlie. "Are they going to be alright?"

The inspector nodded gravely. "Smuggling animals is a horrible business," he said. "And it's not unusual for many to die on the journey. But, thanks to you, they'll be fine. My officers have rounded most of them up safely, and they'll be cared for at a rescue centre until they can be returned to the wild again." He put down his plate and dabbed his mouth with a napkin. "What I don't understand," he said, "is what made you all suspect De Havilland? From what I hear, he's a very well-respected man in these parts."

"It started when we saw the Spectre on the beach," said Joe quickly.

"And then Sherlock bit him," said Charlie.

"But afterwards we saw him talking to Sharkey," said Lucy.

"And then we took the motorboat and overheard Sharkey talking to Mr De Havilland on his yacht," said Joe.

"Right before we planted the tracking device," said Max.

The expression on the inspector's face became increasingly bewildered as the children were talking, until he held up his hands for silence. "Whoa, whoa, wait just a minute," he said. "Spectre? Motorboat? *Tracking device?*" He put down the napkin and took out a notebook and pencil from his inside pocket. "Perhaps you had all better start from the beginning." He glanced over at the sergeant. "And perhaps we should call their parents to come and collect them when we've finished?"

The children let out a collective groan. "Not our parents," said Max. "My mum will go into orbit when she finds out I climbed out of my bedroom window."

"And I'll be running on that treadmill for the rest of my life," said Lucy.

"And my mum's going to be furious that we got Mr De Havilland arrested," said Joe. Then he grinned. "She'll never get invited to the golf club now."

The inspector smiled as he took a seat in one of the armchairs. "Well, I wouldn't worry too much about any of that," he said kindly. "From what I hear, you lot have been real heroes tonight. When your parents learn the true story, I think it's all going to turn out fine."

16

FRIENDS

Max hurried along North Parade, pulling his duffel coat tightly around him. The bitter wind stung his cheeks, and the frozen puddles crackled beneath his feet as he walked. His mum said he must be mad going out on a night like this, but she had still let him go. She seemed to trust him a lot more since they had become famous, he thought.

The sudden snap of cold weather had kept most people inside on Christmas Eve, and Max was alone as he passed gardens filled with large illuminated reindeers, inflatable snowmen, and fairy lights that blinked on and off to the tune of 'Jingle Bells'. But he smiled when he saw a tall and familiar figure walking along the street ahead of him.

"Hey, Luce!" he shouted. "Wait up."

Lucy stopped and turned as Max caught her up. When he saw her up close, Max blinked in amazement. Underneath her overcoat, Lucy was wearing a pretty red dress with a matching scarf, mittens and pumps. Her long black hair was untied from its usual ponytail, and it hung loosely around her shoulders.

"Wow," he said. "You look amazing. I don't think I've ever seen you not wearing a tracksuit."

Lucy smiled and gave him a mock curtsey. "Why, thank you, kind sir," she said. "I do like wearing nice clothes, even if I don't get a chance to wear them very often. And look at you! This is very nice." She leaned forward and straightened his new bow tie, which was blue with large white spots on it.

"Thanks," he said, pleased. "It's not on elastic either. You really have to tie it properly. It was an early Christmas present from Mum. She said I'd better look smart if I was going to be in the papers."

They descended the steps leading down to the beach. "So what do you think this is all about?" asked Lucy as they crossed the soft sand. "All I got was a message from Joe that said, '*Be at the beach hut, 7.00 p.m., Christmas Eve. Wear something posh.*'"

"Same here," said Max. "He wouldn't tell me anything else. But if Joe's planning something, we might all end up in jail by the end of the evening."

They passed the neat rows of colourful beach huts, now shuttered and closed for the winter, until they reached the last hut on the row. There was no sign of anyone about, and the beach hut appeared dark and deserted. "Where's Joe?" asked Lucy. "You don't think he's stood us up, do you?"

"I wouldn't put it past him," said Max. "Try the door."

Lucy mounted the steps and tried the door handle. It opened easily at her touch. She looked at Max quizzically.

"Ladies first," said Max.

Lucy stepped inside cautiously, closely followed by Max. It was pitch dark inside, but the air was warm,

"There's no one in here," hissed Max. "I told you."

There was a soft *click*, and the inside of the little beach hut was suddenly transformed. A string of fairy lights in pink and blue lit up the tiny room and revealed Joe's grinning face, standing by the light switch. "Surprise!" he yelled. He threw another switch, and a tiny Christmas tree in the corner suddenly burst into life with twinkling white lights.

Lucy clapped her hands. "Oh, Joe!" she cried. "It's beautiful in here."

"It's fantastic," said Max, peeling off his coat and taking a seat close to the fire. "I feel like I could spend the whole of Christmas in here."

Joe beamed with delight at the faces of his two friends. He hopped around the tiny space, lighting the oil lamp and putting the kettle on the little gas stove. "I've barely seen any of you since the night the police arrested the smugglers, and I really wanted to get us all together," he said. "And then I remembered that Charlie said she and her mum never celebrated Christmas at home, so I thought we could do something special for her here."

"That's such a lovely thought, Joe," said Lucy. She looked around. "So where is Charlie?"

Joe's face fell. "I don't know," he said. "I sent her a message, but she never replied. Her phone's so old I don't know whether she got it or not, and I don't even know where her house is." He looked at his watch. "But I guess she's not coming now."

They all fell quiet, suddenly feeling the absence of Charlie and Sherlock. "So, anyway," said Joe, breaking the silence, "how did your folks all take it when they got another call from the police?"

"At first I thought my mum was going to go nuclear," said Max. "At one point she even threatened to send me to a boarding school to get me away from 'bad influences'."

"Bad influences?" said Joe.

"She meant you lot," said Max. "But then Inspector Callahan explained how heroic we'd all been capturing the smugglers and how we're all a credit to our families, and she changed completely." He slapped his stomach happily. "She's been giving me extra-large portions all week and telling Saffy that she should take an example from me. It couldn't have worked out better, really."

"Same here," said Lucy. "Dad hit the roof when he first found out. But he calmed down when the inspector spoke to him. Then when the reporters came to our house, they photographed us together, and they described him as an 'Olympic running coach'. I think he was more pleased about that than anything else."

"My mum was furious at first too," said Joe. "She kept going on about 'poor Mr De Havilland', and she said I'd made her a social outcast. She even made Dad come home early from his business trip specially so he could tell me off."

"So what happened?" asked Lucy.

"Well, by the time Dad got home, it was all over the papers," said Joe. "Then all of Mum's set began calling her to hear the story first-hand. She and Dad got invited to the Jackson-Foleys' for mulled wine and mince pies tonight. Mum was over the moon. She's been trying to get an invitation there for ages. Apparently, they're related to royalty." He stuck his nose into the air and made them all laugh by pretending to drink tea with his pinky finger stuck out straight.

"I could get used to being famous," said Max, reclining on the cushions. "Toby Watts and his goons don't dare to touch me now. I walked past them at the bus stop on my way here, and they didn't say a word to me."

"And did you see the papers?" said Joe. He reached into a large bag and slapped a thick wadge of newspaper down onto the table. There were several local papers and even a national edition that all carried a version of the same story about how the children had helped to catch De Havilland and his gang. "'Hero children outwit Jungle Crew'," said Joe, reading from a paper on the top of the pile.

"This one says the police have recommended us for a bravery award," said Lucy. She looked down at her dress. "I'm not sure where I'd pin it though."

"There's a photo of all of us in this one," said Max. "But it makes me look really short."

"I hate to break it to you, Max," said Joe, "but that's not an optical illusion." He opened another paper to a centre-page spread, complete with diagrams of the beach and a picture of De Havilland's yacht. "This one's got a story about how you built the tracking device, Max," he said. "It calls you a 'child genius'."

Max made a show of breathing on his fingernails and then rubbing them on his lapel.

Lucy was reading a longer article in one of the local papers. Her jaw had dropped open, and her eyes opened wide. "Did you see this?" she squeaked. "It's an interview with Creech, the harbourmaster. He says he'd been suspicious of De Havilland all along and that he was the one who called the police and rescued us on the beach."

"The dirty liar!" exclaimed Joe. "Still, it's just like the man to want to get in on the act." He peered over Lucy's shoulder to look at the article. "At least they included all our names," he said. "But I don't think Charlie will like it. They've called her 'Charlotte'."

Lucy put down her paper and sighed. "It's such a shame Charlie didn't come," she said. "It doesn't seem right to be here enjoying ourselves when she's not here. We'd never have solved the mystery if it hadn't been for her and Sherlock."

The others nodded glumly and fell silent again. Then Joe brightened. "Hey, is anyone hungry?" He reached into the bag again and produced a large frying pan. "I thought we could have some bacon and eggs?"

Max and Lucy laughed. "Good grief, Joe," said Lucy. "How much more stuff have you got in that bag?"

Max was squinting into the bag and had pulled out a large packet of bacon and a box of eggs. "Well," he said slowly, "I had three helpings of dinner earlier." Then he grinned. "But that was nearly an hour ago, so, yeah, I could eat bacon and eggs."

Joe jumped up and put the pan on the cooker and started heating the oil. When the kettle boiled, he made more of his speciality lumpy hot chocolate and passed the mugs around. As he was placing Max's mug down on the table, there was the tiniest of scratches at the door. Then the door swung open to reveal Charlie and Sherlock standing in the entrance.

Charlie gave them a small smile. "Is it okay?" she said. "If we come in, I mean? We're not interrupting anything, are we?"

The others stared at her in amazement for a moment, and then Joe cried out, "Charlie! Sherlock! Of course you're not interrupting anything, stupid. I organised this *for you!* So that you could have a real Christmas."

He bounded towards Charlie and gave her a huge hug, lifting her off her feet in the process. Sherlock barked and leapt up onto the benches, where he proceeded to lick Max's and Lucy's faces as though they had been covered in ice cream and he, Sherlock, had been given the very important task of getting it all off.

Charlie looked startled as Joe spun her around. When he put her down, she was pink and breathless. "Wow," she said, looking around at the Christmas tree and the lights. "Do you really mean it? You did all of this for me and Sherlock?"

"It was all Joe's idea," said Lucy. "Isn't it great?"

Charlie agreed it was great and took a seat between Max and Lucy while Joe made her some lumpy hot chocolate. Then he started to fry up the bacon and eggs, filling the cabin with delicious hot smells.

"This is so brilliant," said Max as Joe placed four plates of food on the table and another, smaller plate with two rashers of bacon on the floor for Sherlock. "I'm half starved."

"I thought you only ate an hour ago?" asked Lucy.

"And your point would be?" said Max through a mouthful of eggs.

"I still can't believe you did all this for me and Sherlock," said Charlie, who had not been able to stop staring at the Christmas tree. "I thought...I thought after it was all over and once we'd solved the mystery that you wouldn't want us around anymore."

"Why on earth wouldn't we want you around?" said Joe.

Charlie shrugged. "I don't know. Whenever I meet new people, I usually end up being rude to them or getting angry so that they start hating me. I guess I just never managed to stay friends with anyone this long before." She turned and smiled at each of them in turn.

"Of course we're still friends," said Lucy.

"And heroes," said Joe.

"Don't forget 'child geniuses'," added Max.

"We're all of those things," said Lucy.

"I'll drink to that," said Joe, raising his mug.

They clinked their mugs of lumpy hot chocolate and laughed out loud, recalling their adventures of the last few days. It turned out that Joe had also brought a large carrot cake from the kitchen cupboard at home, which he cut up into five hefty chunks and which Max and Sherlock managed to eat most of. Then Joe had one last surprise.

From the very bottom of his bag he produced four presents wrapped in the sort of untidy, rumpled way that only eleven-year-old boys know how to do. There was a new water bottle for Lucy that she could take on her runs and a stylish new tie for Max. Charlie had a guide book of British birds, and Sherlock had a rawhide bone. He woofed delightedly when Charlie unwrapped it for him and immediately set to chewing it on the rug.

"This has been the best Christmas ever," said Charlie as she hugged her knees in delight. "Thanks so much for being my friends."

"So can we call ourselves a gang now?" said Joe.

"Or how about a crew?" said Max.

"What was it that De Havilland called us?" said Lucy. "Oh, I remember. He said we were like an 'after school detective club'. That's what we should call ourselves."

They all agreed that was an excellent name and sealed it with more hot chocolate and carrot cake until they could barely move. "Oh gosh, is that the time!" said Lucy. "I promised I wouldn't be late. There's still loads of wrapping to do at home."

"Me too," said Max, standing up and stretching.

They packed away the dirty crockery and the remains of the food into Joe's bag and then turned off the Christmas tree lights and filed outside.

"Hey, look at that," said Lucy, staring upwards. The others followed her gaze and saw that thick white flakes of snow were floating down gracefully and settling on the sand. The beach was beginning to turn white.

"It really is a white Christmas," said Joe.

"Let's all promise to meet up in the New Year," said Charlie.

"I'll second that," said Lucy.

"Sure," said Max, patting his belly again. "But let's get Christmas out of the way first, shall we? I have a *lot* of eating to do before then." And they all laughed as they walked arm in arm along the beach in the direction of home.

ABOUT THE AUTHORS

Mark Dawson is the author of the John Milton, Beatrix and Isabella Rose and Soho Noir series.

www.markjdawson.com

Allan Boroughs is a writer and traveller and the author of the 'Legend of Ironheart' and the 'Starless and Black Mysteries' series for children.

www.allanboroughs.com

Freya and Samuel are Mark's kids. They love bicycles, scooters, dogs, rabbits and dinosaurs.

ALSO BY F.S. DAWSON

The Case of the Smuggler's Curse

The Legend of Ragnar's Gold (Coming Soon)

Printed in Great Britain
by Amazon

51470808R00086